LOBSTER, WITH A STRAW

Lovis Johnson

Copyright © 2022 Lovis Johnson

All rights reserved

The characters and events portrayed in this book are fictitious. Any similarity to real persons, living or dead, is coincidental and not intended by the author.

No part of this book may be reproduced, or stored in a retrieval system, or transmitted in any form or by any means, electronic, mechanical, photocopying, recording, or otherwise, without express written permission of the publisher.

ISBN: 9798810503316
Imprint: Independently published

Cover design by: Lovis Johnson
Library of Congress Control Number: 2018675309
Printed in the United States of America

CONTENTS

Title Page	
Copyright	
Chapter 1	1
Chapter 2	13
Chapter 3	26
Chapter 4	37
Chapter 5	47
Chapter 6	56
Chapter 7	65
Chapter 8	78
Chapter 9	97
Chapter 10	115
Chapter 11	123
Chapter 12	135
Chapter 13	146
Epilogue	158
Acknowledgement	171

CHAPTER 1

Some people have the gift to make an entire hall fall silent.

I'm proud to say I can do the same. Only I'm none of those people you're probably thinking of.

Of course, it would be kind of great if it were my stunning looks that make people stop talking mid-sentence, or the beauty of my smile causing them to stare wide-eyed. Sure, I try to keep my appearance as immaculate as possible. Which isn't easy if you don't dress yourself in the morning, shave your own face or brush your own hair. And yes, I've heard a few times that I have a sunny smile (mostly from women over fifty, though). But no, I don't think any of that applies here. I'm pretty certain that those rows and rows of mostly middle-aged, gray-faced men in dark, pin-striped suits aren't turned toward me now in almost perfect silence because of my style in clothing. Neither is it my voice, because I haven't spoken yet and don't really plan to.

Well, there's no point in pretending I don't know perfectly well what it is.

For one thing, there's the wheelchair. The powerchair that slowly moves to the front with a distinct humming sound, following the direction in which my right hand nudges the joystick. And then... there's me. The tall, lanky guy in it, with the stiff limbs locked in weird positions, the incessant shaking and trembling of my body and the involuntary grimaces that appear on my face.

Yep, especially that.

It takes me long enough to maneuver the wheelchair closer to the speaker's table without running it over, that a few people in the room start coughing and fidgeting in their seats, clearly uncomfortable. I'd bet most of them wish by now that they had stayed outside after the coffee break. Well, too late, gentlemen. Now you've got to find a way to get through the next thirty minutes and pretend you're interested in what I have to say. And no, leaving the room now would probably not be considered appropriate, in case you were wondering.

My aide Romina steps forward and moves my twitching right hand from the joystick onto the enormous computer mouse that I use.

And then there's that absolute silence again.

Because if it's not any of that, then it's surely the way I communicate, through a text-to-speech program that reads out loud what I've written to accompany the presentation slides I've prepared. The voice from the speakers is a good one, with perfect articulation I can only dream of, if a little flat and mechanical altogether. All I need to do is advance each slide by pushing my hand down on the computer mouse and then wait for the computer voice to finish its part.

I'll be honest here: it's fairly easy. I mean, working the computer mouse is not the easiest thing in the world for me personally, although probably a two-year-old could do it. But all in all, it's not a heavy task and it gives me the opportunity to study the audience. Provided my neck and head don't decide of their own volition that the ceiling is way more interesting. But when I'm not having an absolutely shitty day, I usually get to watch the faces of the people in front of me.

And this is when it gets really interesting.

Because it always starts out the same. In the beginning, almost half of the audience is still focused on me instead of on the slides. My writhing body strapped into the chair seems to magically attract stares. Seriously, I bet every talk show host would wish for such an effect. There is the open, oblivious stare, paired with a slightly hanging mouth (not so unlike mine, thank you very much). The kind of self-conscious nervous gaze that jumps all over the place in fascination, from my crossed, trembling legs to my heavily jerking left arm and back to the constantly shifting grimaces on my face. And then there's the ashamed glimpse out of the corner of the eye and the poorly suppressed panic, paired with relief that seems to say "Fuck man, I'm so glad that's not me."

That one's the worst, seriously.

Sometimes people realize I notice them looking and then they get all kinds of flustered. A few at least have the decency to look guilty, while others do their best to pretend they didn't notice me in the first place.

Well, try to convince someone else.

Only after a certain while, several slides into the presentation, does the picture change. I can see frowns appearing on a few faces and eyebrows lifted in mild surprise. They're the signs of people slowly catching on. And eventually the dead silence that feels like a wall in front of me crumbles with people leaning in to their neighbors and quiet whispers of disbelief filling the room. It's always like this. The content of my presentation usually takes a while to seep into brains that were rather preoccupied with staring at me only a second ago. I'm well aware that people simply need a moment to realize that what I'm talking about may be actually interesting to them.

At this time I usually pause a few extra seconds to give everyone the chance to get on board before resuming.

Toward the end of the presentation the room has turned to a state of attentive concentration and every single person watching the slides behind me. Except, the last slide causes a bit of a disruption with the request for yes-and-no questions only and the remark that all other questions will be answered via email. Now everyone is reminded that there's a reason they just listened to thirty minutes of lifeless recorded words strung together into sentences.

In case they forgot.

I manage to pull my hand back from the computer mouse and settle it on the armrest where it stays, fingers trembling a bit, signaling the end of the talk. The applause that follows is appreciative, and I try to look grateful and not move too weirdly (ha!) while all eyes are on me. Everyone knows it's not over yet and I steel my back, mentally preparing myself for the round of questions. Not that trying to sit up straighter actually has much effect on the twisted way I'm slumped in my wheelchair.

"On slide 32 you showed Moor's relation applied to your case. Is it right that this can also be seen as a supportive argument for reversal of inhibition?"

I nod, pleasantly surprised. An excellent observation indeed. Obviously, I didn't go into details because of time constraints but the man with the ridiculous bow-tie and friendly round face is completely right. I try to smile thankfully at him as he sits down again, but I don't think I'm successful.

A red-haired guy gets up and asks while looking at his notes instead of at me: "Would you say that your method is superior to the one presented in a recent study by Heynes?"

My shoulder twitches and my right knee jumps up a bit, undecided. I think I showed plenty of evidence that the method I presented is fairly good, but it certainly depends on the details. I didn't do direct comparisons with Heynes' method, which targets a much more specific application, and don't want to make any statements regarding transferability of our work in this early stage yet.

But of course there's no time for me to communicate that.

"Wouldn't this all mean that we've been wasting money for years?"

I turn my head on the headrest to look at the man asking the question, a balding guy with a thick mustache who sat in the front row to the right. I pause and then nod, attempting to smile apologetically. This draws a few chuckles from the audience.

The man isn't finished yet, though. "But won't conditions change in the future?"

'Slide 44,' I think. Honestly, when you fall asleep during a talk, why would you ask questions afterward? I stare at the man, my left foot rattling against the footrest and my arm jerking outward a few times. The mustache trembles as the guy stares back and when he doesn't get any other reaction he flushes pink and hurriedly sits down again.

An excellent idea.

A few more reasonable questions follow and I shake my head or nod in answer. Sometimes I kind of gesture to my assistant and she notes down a more complex question for me to answer via email later.

An older guy with a gray suit and cropped hair style gets up from his chair and takes the microphone in hand. "Theodore Hebert." He doesn't state his affiliation as if that much should be obvious. I have never met him before in person, but that doesn't mean anything since I don't mingle much. His name jogs my memory, though. He played some part in the team initially trying to come up with a solution to the problem I occupied my recent years of research with. I'm sure he can't be happy about having competition in this field, especially since I'm partly contradicting their work, and I almost feel a little bad for him.

Almost.

"What are the limitations of your work?" Hebert asks.

"Please phrase your question as a yes-no question or send an email later," Romina reminds him.

The guy barely glances at Romina, but his lip twitches in annoyance. "Ah, how *very convenient...*" he mutters under his breath. Then he goes on as if he hadn't heard her. "To be honest, I highly doubt that such a simple solution should be enough to solve a years-old problem. I'm sorry to say this but..."

He definitely isn't sorry, based on the spiteful glint in his eyes.

"...maybe you should have tested your hypothesis more thoroughly."

That's not really a question at all and the guy's barely veiled accusation causes murmurs to erupt throughout the hall. I lift the fingers of my right hand a fraction before Romina can authorize the next question. I wish with all my heart I could engage in a real discussion here, and tell this guy that we are well aware of the limitations of our work, that our results are genuine and our hypothesis well tested, as I have shown during my talk for everyone to see who is willing to understand. But I can't, not really. I don't want to leave it like that, though. By now the hall is buzzing with excited chatter, everyone wanting to weigh in with their opinion, and the guy, Hebert, sits down again, smiling smugly at his seat neighbor, obviously pleased with himself.

The technician fixed a microphone to the front of my shirt, although Romina told him it wasn't necessary. I might as well try to put it to some use.

"E..." My throat is dry from the air-conditioning and the fact that I haven't attempted to speak for a while. I swallow, which takes some time, and then start again. "E. F. ... Schu... macher..." I choke out and the hall falls dead silent again.

The thing is, my articulation really is bad. It's like my tongue has a life of its own and more often than not my jaw is clamped shut or refusing to close at the appropriate occasion. A mix of all of that is just what is happening right now and although I tried to bring across not much more than a word I didn't succeed, apparently.

Everyone is staring at me.

"Uh... excuse me?" Hebert's face is perplexed.

I turn my head to look at Romina, grimacing helplessly, and she translates for me. "Mr. Hallman said: E. F. Schumacher," she tells the audience. Bless her, she really is gold. She has worked for me for almost four years now and she knows to read me even when I myself wouldn't understand what comes out of my mouth.

Hebert's frown stays. "Schumacher?" he repeats.

From the back someone starts reciting the beginning of the famous quote by the statistician and economist: "Any intelligent fool can make things bigger and more complex..." and somewhere in the audience people chuckle, one or two even applauding a little.

All in all, the rest of the question round goes surprisingly well and that's the end of today's session. The legs of metal chairs scrape over the floor and chatter bubbles up around me as people stream out of the room. A few brave ones detour to walk past the speaker's table and politely congratulate me on my talk. I sit and kind of nod at them and try to give my best smile, which is more or less exactly all I can do on my own. Romina is packing up my laptop and the mouse, and handing out my business cards to people whose questions weren't answered. She hasn't set up my talker for me to reach yet. Not that most people are patient enough to wait for me to type in a response anyway, which is the reason why I don't use it in question rounds.

"Will we meet you at dinner tonight?"

I look up to recognize the guy with the bow-tie from the question round. He has a friendly, although slightly anxious smile. Since he's the only person brave enough to start an actual conversation with me, I have to give him some credit though.

I pause. I'd like to give him a positive answer but the conference dinner is scheduled to last well into the evening. When the mere act of getting into bed involves a Hoyer lift, your entire nighttime routine is a bit more excessive than for other people. I've spent a night in the hotel room already and it has worked out okay, but my aide and I are both still getting used to the foreign equipment. Everything takes longer than it would normally and even without that it would take forever. Plus I can't swallow food that hasn't gone through a blender before, and I'm not entirely sure that I want to be spoon-fed right in front of those people that I've just painstakingly convinced that I'm more than an object of pity.

The black-haired man is getting visibly flustered when he can't read a response in my erratic movements, but he's still smiling. "Is that a no?" He laughs, still nervous.

I try shrugging and my legs go into more severe spasms, lifting up from the footrest.

"Uh… A maybe?" The guy ventures.

I nod, relieved he got that.

"Mr. Hallman?"

I manage to turn my head to the left. A man with a large red face is approaching me from the side, holding pen and paper in one hand while the other is thrust out to me, offering a handshake. "My name is Kent Bonde. I'm thrilled to make your acquaintance."

Let's face it: here I am, needing help in moving my hand from the joystick of my wheelchair to the table in front of me. How on earth would anyone think that I could shake hands? Sure, I'd really like to be able to since it's such a frequent social gesture. But if I attempted grabbing that guy's hand I'd probably end up slapping his arm instead, if I even succeeded in getting anywhere near it. Though, thinking about it, hitting him is maybe not such a bad option.

Instead I force myself to smile until the man, Kent, finally realizes his faux-pas. His arm falls to his side again and he coughs uncomfortably. He hurriedly introduces himself as a reporter of a local magazine, and when he doesn't receive any response to that save for a dizzying wiggle of my head, he leaves with a promise to write an email.

Which he probably won't ever write, but I find that I don't care at all.

Just then I hear a short chuckle and look up again. A woman is standing in front of me.

And well...

She's just...

Gorgeous.

Just so that you understand: one, her gender alone makes her stand out in the sea of men filing out of the room behind her; two, she's younger than me by a couple of years and thus much younger than the average person attending this event; and three... she apparently wants to talk to me. Which, all in all, makes her about a hundred times more interesting than most people in the room.

And yes, she's attractive.

Like... holy shit, she's so out of my league it's almost ridiculous. Her long, dark brown hair is held back by a red hairband and flows in waves over her shoulders, her brown eyes are those large, deer-like ones that make you want to marry her on the spot, and her nose is cute with freckles that the bit of makeup she's wearing fails to conceal. Her smile is confident and friendly, and her gaze rests steadily on my face instead of watching one of my restlessly moving limbs, making me instantly like her.

"My name is Lauren Brooks," she says. Her voice is lively and clear and it sends shivers down my spine. "I totally loved your talk!"

I wonder how I could miss her in the audience before and conclude that she must have sat in the front to the left-hand side of the audience, out of my field of vision.

"Um... I really don't want to be a bother but if you have time...?" Lauren gestures with the closed laptop she clutches in her hands, which gives me an excuse to take in her entire appearance. She's wearing a cute short dress, blue with a red ribbon around her waist – maybe a touch too cute for a serious event like this – and matching red pumps.

I must admit: she's absolutely killing that look.

Where's Romina? I try to locate my aide but she seems swarmed by people. Shit. Being able to communicate would be freaking awesome right now.

Lauren watches me. She seems a bit hesitant but not uncomfortable, clears her throat and then goes on, taking my silence as approval. "I work in a field related to yours," she says, "and I was wondering if you'd be willing to have a look at my current project... I think it's quite interesting but I'm feeling a bit stuck at the moment and I really just hoped you'd maybe have an idea that will help me go on. With you being an absolute expert in this."

If she goes on like this I fear I'm going to blush, so I nod my head quickly to speed things on.

Lauren puts her laptop on the slightly raised speaker's table in front of me, opens it and sits on the table's surface next to it.

It kind of makes sense. There's no chair, since the only one was removed to make space for my wheelchair. So it's only natural for her to sit on the desk. But I'm not sure if Lauren knows just how far the skirt of her dress has raked up her long thighs as she crossed her legs and that my eyes are almost perfectly on level with her crotch now. I catch a glimpse of her red satin slip for a split second and I quickly try to look somewhere else.

Because I have manners. Some.

Just to land accidentally on her boobs that are bouncing in front of my face as she leans forward over the screen. My cock gives a very distinct twitch in my pants and I stifle a groan.

Fuck.

I need to pull myself together or this is going to be an embarrassing disaster.

Lauren opens a presentation and shows me a few videos and illustrations, continuing to lean over to me, her hair falling forward and a wave of her perfume clouding my senses.

Jesus F... Christ, is this girl entirely oblivious of her effect or is she doing it on purpose?

Well, it's not like I'm a virgin. But believe me, when you're like me, dating is no picnic. I've had a few brief relationships, with attraction mostly on the intellectual level. But I *do* have physical needs (in case you were wondering) and in that field it definitely gets hairy. I mean, have you ever tried flirting using a talker? Believe me, the computer voice just sucks at doing sultry. Not to mention that thanks to my condition I'm almost exclusively on the receiving side of pleasure. I wish it were different, but... I have the success rate of a drunken truck driver performing an abdominal surgery blind. I can't even get myself off most of the time, how do you expect me to master such a fickle thing as a vagina?

I can't come up with any reason why Lauren would throw her feminine charms into my twitching face and conclude that she's probably just very, very cute and very, very dumb.

And somehow very intelligent at the same time, as it seems. I don't immediately recognize the logo of her university on her first slide although I figure from the looks of it that it must be a small one maybe farther south. Nevertheless, her results are stunning. It takes only a few minutes for me to see the potential in her work, she's got a unique angle on the topic and my professional interest soars. As she continues to narrate her thoughts to me, several ideas start to form in my head and without me having to do anything more I can see the entire project gaining shape. Thankfully the distraction also turns my horniness down to a more bearable level.

Because a hard-on when there's zero you can do about it... sucks. Absolutely no pun intended.

A short sound in the back of my throat causes Lauren to stop. I angle the wheelchair to the side a bit by knocking my hand against the joystick, slipping out of Lauren's radius of influence at the same time. "Romina? Can I get you for a sec?"

My aide's name is impossible for me to pronounce right but the vocals I can do and there are few words with the same sequence that it can be confused with. Plus, the ugly sound of my voice itself is unmistakable. I swear, if you've heard it once it'll probably haunt you forever.

Romina turns from where she has spoken to a handful of people loitering behind, notes down something on the pad in her hand and gestures at them in goodbye, smiling in a friendly but definite way. They nod hurriedly and look past her and at me, stunned. Probably they heard me trying to speak a full sentence as well. One of them pulls at the sleeve of the jacket of one of the others, all the while not taking his gaze off me, and another stumbles over his own feet attempting to walk to the exit while staring back at me at the same time.

"Patrick, I'm so sorry, I totally forgot you there for a minute!" Romina apologizes as she approaches quickly, waving the notepad. "There will be hundreds of mails I'm afraid."

"I'm already looking forward to it," I say, aiming for dry humor. Oh, how I sometimes wish my voice could drip sarcasm. "You couldn't have told them that it's not worth the effort because... let's see... I'd die soon or something?"

Romina grins and chuckles. We've got a good dynamic between us, I think. She's in fact my favorite aide to bring to events like these, simply because she takes everything in stride and is generally not overly impressed by the entire hubbub that comes with professional conferences. "Talker?" she asks, wiping my chin quickly with a tissue at the same time. Spit? Shit...

I notice Lauren has gone still and stares at us, puzzled.

Of course. To anyone who hasn't known me for as long as Romina has our conversation must sound quite weird. Speaking is hard for me and very exhausting when I have to concentrate on getting as much right as possible. With Romina I know that she even understands me when I don't put so much effort into it and so I let my articulation slack when talking to her. Like.... a lot. Which results in utter garbled mess coming out of my mouth if anything at all, while Romina answers just normally. Because somehow she actually understands me. I don't know how she does it; it's probably a combination of figuring out the consonants that I can do well and sensing those I usually trash, knowing to tell actual vocals apart from the random sounds I make and filling in the words that I swallowed entirely by whatever fits best based on context. As I told you, she's amazing.

The only other people with this talent are my parents and my brother. And they've had more than thirty years of training.

I smile reassuringly at Lauren while Romina adjusts the screen that is attached to my right armrest and was folded away previously to make it easier for me to reach the laptop mouse on the table.

"I'm going to put the equipment back into the speaker's room," Romina says and places my hand on the joystick. "Are you good here?"

I jerk my head into a nod and my aide leaves the room with my laptop and her notes in a bag.

Am I good? I dare to look at Lauren who smiles at me and tucks a strand of her beautiful hair behind her ear. Her long, crossed legs are slightly swinging back and forth under the table, making me all dizzy. She clears her throat and looks at me expectantly.

No, I'm not exactly sure I'm good.

CHAPTER 2

Lauren and I are alone now and I have to admit I grow a bit nervous, busying myself with the talker. I type with the knuckles of my right hand, by leaning my fist to the side from the position of the joystick. I can only reach half of the screen that way and need to scroll through some of the alphabet to type anything. The word prediction algorithm is a blessing. "Slide 3," the computer voice reads.

Lauren changes her slides to the correct number.

"Graph on the right. Conclusive with statement B on slide 6?"

Lauren is fast in decoding the stunted sentences I use and she understands immediately. "Oh! I hadn't thought about this… but… yes, that's a great idea!" Her eyes light up. "So what about —"

We dive into a discussion of different methods and all kinds of details, and, bit by bit, we develop a strategy to help her move her work forward. Somehow our entire conversation flows easily, much easier than is usually the case with strangers. Lauren is endlessly patient with me composing the sentences on the screen and she doesn't seem to mind when I get distracted by spasms for a few seconds. But anyway there isn't much I need to say once I've started the ball rolling. Lauren is indeed very good at what she does and so she does most of the talking. All I need to do is give a few hints and suggestions.

In the end Lauren thanks me a thousand times, her eyes sparkling with excitement. Her enthusiasm is contagious and I can't help but smile at her. She's so much in her own headspace in this moment, it reminds me of myself a couple of years ago.

"I'd maybe need to find more data to support this argument but yes… it could work. Thank you so much Mr.—"

"Patrick." My name is on speed dial, so to say.

"Thanks, Patrick."

"I'm very excited to hear about your progress." I mean it. She's doing great work.

Lauren beams happily. "I'll make sure to inform you. I suppose I can find your contact data online?"

I nod. The company's website should pop up whenever someone searches my name online.

"It was very kind of you to help me, Patrick." Lauren smiles at me, her lips cherry red and full.

I swallow laboriously, warmth creeping into my face as I watch her. Lauren is damn beautiful and I apparently really need it bad. Unbidden, the idea of what her body looks like underneath her cute blue dress creeps into my mind and I wonder how those amazing lips would taste. The thought alone has my arousal peak again, which unfortunately cranks up my spasms. My arms and hands stiffen and keep me from typing on the screen.

Lauren continues smiling at me when my reply is no more than a few completely unintentional grunts as my neck flexes abruptly and my head bounces against the headrest. She closes the laptop, wedges it under her arm and hops off the table. "I'd be honored if we could continue this conversation during dinner tonight," she says. As she steps past me her hand brushes along my arm, if on purpose I can't really tell. Still being in the middle of an episode I jump in surprise, reflexively gasping.

And choke on my own spit.

That happens sometimes. I have difficulties swallowing or controlling my tongue and I can't cough well either. Usually it's not immediately dangerous and just takes a few wheezing attempts until I can breathe normally again. If you want to call it normal, because I make all kinds of sounds just by breathing.

I can see Lauren is concerned as she watches me struggle for air but thankfully she doesn't freak out. Someone crying for an ambulance now is all I need. Not that it would be a first, though.

"Are you, um... okay?"

I nod as soon as I've taken a few rattling breaths, not meeting Lauren's eyes. Very sexy, Patrick. Very. "Sorry," I type, feeling my cheeks heat again.

Lauren laughs merrily. She has a beautiful laugh, loud and rich. "No worries. I have to apologize for being so pushy."

"You don't have to," the computer voice reads after a while. Did I mention I'm slow at typing?

Lauren giggles. "Okay, I'm glad to hear that. About dinner... does that mean you—"

"So, all done!"

Romina has returned and approaches us quickly, only regarding Lauren with a fleeting glance. "Are you ready, Patrick?" She gesticulates to the exit.

I groan inwardly. I just had a couple of minutes alone with a woman and all but thoroughly managed to make an idiot out of myself.

To my surprise, Lauren doesn't seem to think that or if she does, she doesn't seem to care, because she acts quickly. "If we hurry we might get a table together," she says and turns to me with her eyebrows lifted.

Romina frowns. "A table?"

"At the conference dinner," Lauren clarifies.

I look at the two women towering over me and hesitate a second. I hadn't planned to attend the conference dinner and I'm really reluctant to go. There will be a large number of influential people present and I loathe being on display in general, but eating is my absolutely weakest point by far.

But then I nod. How can I say no to Lauren? I'd try to pull an entire lobster through a straw if it meant sharing a few more minutes with her.

Lauren beams happily at me and that alone convinces me that I've made the right decision.

"Oh..." Romina's expression changes to somewhat disapproving. "In that case, I need to make arrangements with the kitchen."

"I'm sorry," I hurriedly apologize to her, my head lolling

around. I really can't have my aide be pissed off at me. "I know I hadn't planned to go tonight but... um... plans have changed. If it's too much effort, though, we can go back to the hotel and—"

Romina shakes her head, eyes distant. Probably she's already going through the list of things she needs to inform people about. Enough space for the chair and for her at my side, straws for the drinks and blended food. I know it's a lot on short notice but I have faith that she'll manage. "Okay," she finally says. "I'm going to head over and make sure everything is ready for you, alright? And you... uh..." For a second Romina seems a little overwhelmed because she can't possibly take me along but also can't leave me alone for too long.

"We'll have drinks in the foyer," Lauren says. As Romina and I spoke she has watched me with her eyebrows lifted but I've subtly ignored her. My terrible speech, unintelligible to most, can be an advantage sometimes. "And then search for a table."

"Okay...?" Romina looks at me and I nod.

It's okay, really. I know my aide doesn't like the idea of leaving me alone with a stranger and to be frank, neither do I. Lauren is nice but she has no experience with me. It isn't like I come with an operations manual tacked to my forehead, but maybe I should. I'm pretty sure I am going to survive, though. I mean, relatively sure. Provided I manage to forget all about Lauren's beauty and concentrate on the basic necessities, like breathing correctly and just generally not embarrassing myself. That'd be awesome.

We all exit the conference room, Romina hurrying in front of us and Lauren walking slower next to my humming wheelchair. It's rigged to go rather slowly, since I don't have the best command over the joystick, and Romina soon vanishes from my field of vision. The dining hall and the foyer are located two more floors up in the conference building and people are streaming up the broad stairs and the two sets of escalators. I lead the way in front of Lauren away from the main crowd, toward the elevators.

There's too much noise and I can't type while steering the

powerchair anyway, so we don't talk. The area in front of the elevators is occupied by a bunch of people who haven't yet given up on the hope that the elevators will bring them faster to the desired drinks than the stairs. Lauren and I stop at the edge of it, waiting for our turn.

"Did you visit Uluru on holidays?" I ask her. As always, a few people standing next to us turn around upon hearing the computer voice of the talker. It's not so much different from a human's voice but it's not as perfect as to fool anyone. It's decidedly better than my own voice, though.

As usual I try my best to ignore everyone.

Lauren chuckles surprised. "How do you know?"

"Your wallpaper." I caught a glimpse at the photo of her in front of the massive red rock formation in the Australian desert before she closed her laptop.

Lauren laughs, a bright and refreshing sound, and shakes her head. "No, that was work-related. Still a great spot. Have you been there?"

I shake my head. Although I'm a frequent flyer, I've never actually undertaken such a long flight. It's possible for me with some major planning effort in advance, I guess, and in fact I'd like to visit Australia one time. But so far I've been lacking the motivation to go to the trouble.

The elevator arrives with a ding and the doors open. It's empty. A handful of people detach from the waiting crowd and walk inside. The rest hesitate, some turning to look at me expectantly. It's clear we won't all fit inside. I'd wait for my turn like everyone else but I'm not going to discuss this now, so I tilt the joystick forward and maneuver the powerchair into the small cubicle. Once I'm in, there's hardly space for an additional person. Lauren manages to squeeze in behind me and then the doors close.

The ride up is quiet except for my left dress shoe clanging against the footrest rhythmically. It's an awkward situation with the people in the elevator in front of me giving their best not to stare. I still catch a few quickly glancing my way before they direct their gazes over my head again. I can't blame them. I'm too much of an attraction not to be watched.

Thankfully it's over quickly. Lauren steps out of the elevator first and I steer the powerchair out backward, hoping that people have made enough room for me. Sometimes there's a mirror attached to the elevator wall opposite of the doors and angled in on top. I bet you've never noticed. Well, its purpose would come in handy for me now but of course this elevator has no such thing to help me see what's behind me. Thankfully, I manage not to run over anyone's feet – or if I do no one is complaining – and Lauren and I try to get out of the crowd.

This level of the conference center is mostly wide, carpeted space, with a number of high tables placed in rows parallel to the long side of the building. The walls are glass with the view going out to the business buildings across the street. As soon as we've found a calm spot at the edge of the crowd in the hall, Lauren tells me about her field work near Uluru. She's full of funny anecdotes involving camping in the desert and cranky researchers who spend most of their time in the outback. In some disturbing detail she tells me about their dinner specialty of honey ants and witchetty grubs, and I make a face, utterly disgusted. Lauren laughs at it.

"Oh, and it gets so cold during nights. We used to do one minute of jumping jacks before we went to bed. Everyone in a circle around the campfire."

That certainly sounds hilarious and, damn, now I'm picturing her in a very short nightdress dancing under the night sky.

"It was a great time but also… You know, with fieldwork, it always depends a lot on the people. It was amazing because it was a fun team to work with. Everyone was just damn nice, even to a noob like me." She grins at me and shrugs. "I know how to make a mean stew, though, so maybe that was why." She laughs beautifully. "I can imagine it could be horrible if you're forced to live and work 24/7 with a bunch of jackasses, though…"

I nod, my legs quivering. "I guess so," I type. "I'll never forget being snowed in for a while with a few guys in Canada. That's when you get to know a whole new side of your team. It was invaluable."

Lauren's eyes light up. "You do fieldwork?" The surprise is evident in her voice. Almost immediately after she says that her eyes widen and her cheeks turn a light shade of pink. "Um, I mean... geez, I'm sorry, I made assumptions..."

I chuckle. "It's okay. Obviously I'm no Indiana Jones," the talker says.

"Thank god, though" Lauren mumbles. She turns a bit redder than before upon that.

I squint at her, mildly surprised. Don't all girls dream of a smart, muscled adventurer who carries them in his strong arms over a river foaming with giant crocodiles? Or whatever it is that Indiana Jones does.

I clear my throat and almost forget to use the talker. "I was only checking in on one of our projects and definitely didn't intend to stay that long," I explain my short encounter with fieldwork. I still remember the resentment toward my brother when I realized I'd be forced to stay for much longer than planned. He had made me go in the first place, although trips like these are more his job. I prefer staying behind my laptop in well air-conditioned buildings in large cities with a wide range of good, accessible hotels. In the end, spending two weeks in a rather remote camp in the wild, almost skin to skin with the other workers was probably an unforgettable experience for everyone. But to be fair, it was far less horrible than I'd expected it to be and I made friends for life. Not that I'm keen on a repetition, though.

"Oh look at that! Champagne for you as well?" Lauren picks up two glasses from the tray of a passing waiter before I have a chance to answer.

I can't hold a glass in my hands. That much might be obvious. And I can't drink well from any glass because of the same reason that causes me to choke on my own spit and inhibits my speech.

"Cheers." Lauren clinks the two glasses in her hands together and sips from hers. "Good stuff. You too?"

I suppress a sigh because I don't want to explain myself. Hell, I can always pretend I'm taking a sip. Seriously, what can go wrong. I nod and Lauren lifts the second glass to my lips.

Apparently a lot can go wrong.

The moment the glass touches my lips my head jerks to the side and my left arm drives outward, knocking Lauren squarely into the stomach. She yelps, more taken by surprise than in pain, or at least that's what I hope because I'm not very strong, and loses her grip around the stem. Thankfully the champagne glass doesn't fall to the floor and shatters, but instead lands in my lap, where the cold, sparkling liquid washes all over my shirt and pants, hissing softly.

"Shit..." Lauren stares at me, wide-eyed and holding her hands up. "Fuck..." She clasps one hand over her mouth immediately. "I mean... sorry, uh... Oh my god, I'm such a klutz!"

I look at her shocked (and, impossibly, still cute) expression and... start to laugh. Here we are, standing in a hall full of perfectly dressed people that we both desperately want to impress, and I just took a shower in possibly very expensive champagne. At least the glass is still intact.

Lauren stares at me, a bit bewildered no doubt by the sound of my laughter that honest to god resembles a donkey's cry, but then she joins in. We both try to keep it quiet but still a few people turn around to stare at us before hurriedly pretending they didn't notice anything.

Sometimes there are perks to being me.

Lauren carefully picks up the empty glass from my lap, grinning and blinking away tears of joy. "Geez... I should really wear a sign. Attention! Catastrophic person! Don't get near." She giggles, her eyes sparkling as they lock with mine.

I chuckle, a bit out of breath, and find that in fact I don't agree with her at all. I'd like to be as close to her as possible, regardless of whatever liquid she pours over my head. Especially if it makes her laugh like that.

Lauren turns to a set-back corner of the room, with two empty tables and a view to the busy street below us. I follow her, glad to get away from the prying eyes of the masses. I can feel spit leaking out at the corner of my mouth and subtly try to remove it as I join Lauren, merely succeeding in my left arm only narrowly missing her this time. Well, no chance here. My legs go into spasm again and the movement causes the champagne that hasn't leaked into my clothes yet to spread further.

"Okay, wait..." Lauren grabs a handful of napkins from the nearest table. She dabs with the tissue at my shirt. Where the liquid has seeped in, the bright blue color of my shirt has darkened. "Don't move. Uh... geez. Sorry."

She looks at me with wide eyes, mortified, and I burst out into laughter again. No one has ever had the guts to tell me to stop moving. I'm shaking so much with half-suppressed laughter I can't even access my talker anymore, tears streaming over my face. Lauren stops cleaning my clothes and buries her head in her hands with a low groan, her shoulders jumping with the giggles.

When we both have some control again, Lauren crouches down in front of me and presses the napkins onto the wet patches in my lap.

So here's the thing. If you're notoriously underfucked and a beautiful woman rubs her hands over your pants near your private parts, there's zero you can do to prevent a reaction. Like, not even your best image of your math teacher naked or whatever turns you off. It won't work. Because nature is stronger.

I react instantly, knock my right fist against the joystick and back away from Lauren before she can notice my predicament. "It's fine," I drawl, not daring to look up at her, my cheeks burning. This really isn't what I need right now. Or maybe it kind of is, in fact. But it's definitely the wrong time and place for it.

"Um..."

Right, she doesn't understand me. I force my hand to lean over to the talker. "It's okay. Don't bother with the champagne. It's not your fault."

Lauren is silent next to me. I still don't manage to look

properly at her but this time it's because of tight muscles in my neck forcing my head to turn down awkwardly. "Sorry," I add in my computer voice. The word is still saved among "recently used". It seems to be the word of the evening.

Lauren shifts uneasily.

Is she pissed off at me? I probably came across like some kind of dick, refusing her help in cleaning my clothes. God, why did I have to fuck it up? I'm just terrible at this, I guess. I'd give everything to be able to vanish right now. If I attempted to leave, though, I probably wouldn't even make it out of the building on my own because I can't open doors or push buttons in an elevator. Although it's always the case wherever I go, it's never been clearer to me than now that I'm literally trapped in here.

I shouldn't have gone anywhere without Romina, I realize.

Lauren swallows nervously and steps a bit closer, tentatively as if I might bite, her perfume torturing my nose with its pleasantness. Why is she still here? It'd be a piece of cake for *her* to walk away – as far as I know, Lauren shouldn't have any problems with opening doors. My growing anger gets ramped up even more when I realize she probably wants to leave but feels responsible for me and doesn't dare to leave me alone. Geez, I'm not completely helpless, I can survive very well without an assistant for a while. Okay, not for a long while, I guess, and not particularly well. But it's not like I need Lauren to stay for me.

I've just started to type that last part when Lauren clears her throat. The muscles in my neck finally loosen up enough to allow me to look up at her. Lauren's cheeks are almost as pink as mine probably are and her eyes are strangely wide. What's going on with her? "No, I should apologize..." she whispers and blinks. "I'm... That was... I'm sorry."

I stare at her, my throat going instantly dry as her glazed-over eyes meet mine. My gaze is drawn to her hand still holding the napkins and for a split second I wonder how it would be to reach out and take hold of it. I could maybe feel the pulse racing under her skin, confirm her heart beats in her throat just as wildly as mine does. My arm moves, but instead of taking her hand in mine it simply slides from the armrest while my left fist snaps to my chest with a soft thud. I can't suppress a groan as a wicked spasm contorts my face.

Damn it.

Definitely not the right time for an embarrassing attack.

My legs fold tighter at the knees and lift off the footrest, while my upper body starts shaking against the support of my wheelchair. I don't try to fight it because I know there's no point, it's better to let the spasm take its course. I hear Lauren gasp above me and my heart sinks. That's probably it for me now. Lauren won't want to put up with something like this. I can't blame her, I'm pretty sure I look ridiculous when my muscles lock up in one of those more severe storms, my eyes roaming around trying to counteract the shaking. I don't think anyone can take me seriously who has seen that.

If they ever did take me seriously before.

Lauren makes a muffled sound and steps closer, her eyes huge and timid. Her full lips part and I can see her chest heaving under the fabric of her dress. Surprisingly, she doesn't look like she wants to leave. If I had the momentary control to move my arm in a direction I wanted it to be, I'm pretty sure I could actually touch her because she's much closer than she's ever been before. Lauren exhales and I can feel the air moving over my cheeks. I can barely make sense of what is going on, my body is buzzing and I feel a bit dizzy. That must be the reason for believing that for one second it looks like Lauren is bending down to me and—

"Okay, everything's ready!"

Lauren startles and turns around abruptly. A whimper of protest dies in my throat with the instant reminder where we are and that we're not alone, not by any means.

Romina makes her way through the crowd, waving, and then stops in front of us, grinning triumphantly. "I got a table for all of us!"

Well, if there's ever been bad timing… Just a few minutes ago I would've praised Romina's arrival at the scene. But now…

"Oh... uh... that's good," Lauren squeaks and tucks back strands of hair that have fallen into her face. She smiles at Romina and balls the napkins in her hands. "We haven't had time to... uh... search for a table yet."

We haven't had time for that and for whatever was about to take place right there...

Romina leans down to check on me and then hesitates, pulling her eyebrows together. "What happened here?" She has noticed the wet patches on my shirt and pants.

I can't speak with my jaw still painfully locked and I can't access the talker at the moment, either, but I don't need to because Lauren is acting quickly. "I spilled my champagne," she explains, grinning rather convincingly. "Stupid me, huh?" She titters and waves the empty glass of champagne through the air.

Romina makes a noncommittal sound in the back of her throat and bends down to place my trembling right hand on the joystick. The muscles in my arm are too tight though, so it just slides back into my lap again, fingers twitching.

Romina's eyes darken a bit with understanding and she studies my screwed-up face. "Leave?" her lips form the silent question. She knows I hate being in public when I'm having a bad time with my body.

I shake my head minutely and exhale slowly. This will be over in a bit, or at least I desperately hope so. Otherwise I'm not sure I'll be able to down a single spoon of food, let alone communicate properly, and that would mean missing out on getting to know more about Lauren altogether.

Romina reads my pleading gaze correctly. "We'll give it a minute," she says, and gently squeezes my quivering arm that is folded over my chest.

I catch Lauren throwing a furtive glance at me as Romina doesn't watch, her cheeks still a little pink. She bites on her lips and it makes a warm shiver run down my spine.

So I haven't been absolutely wrong. She felt something, too.

When the foyer has almost emptied, I gain back some limited amount of control over my body and manage to steer the powerchair to the large open doors leading into the dining hall. As we go through, Romina turns around to me and lifts her eyebrows. She gives me an inquiring look, pointing with her head to Lauren who walks in the front.

My brain is still a bit foggy and my muscles are only very slowly returning to their normal state of stiffness, so I shrug at Romina as best as I can and choose to say... nothing.

CHAPTER 3

I know that while most people might be fooled, Romina isn't so easily deceived. I don't know if she suspects that there's something going on between Lauren and me but I'd bet my right arm she will soon. And my right arm is my good one, in case that may not have been obvious to you.

Romina and I are pretty close, by necessity, and she knows every detail of my romantic relationships. Probably she even remembers every single time I had sex in the past because she'd been there, at least at the beginning. Plus, the occasions weren't so frequent that you'd lose count. Thankfully my aide has always been supportive of me and I can only hope she's going to continue to be so.

We enter the dining hall among a surge of equally hungry conference participants. Usually I'd prefer a table near the entrance and to the side, so that I don't have to navigate the wheelchair through a maze of chairs, fallen jackets, purses and people still milling around. However, a table like this needs preparation time.

"The best we got is over there," Romina says. She points to a table in the middle section of the room. At least it's to the side so I won't be the total focus of the room. The tables closer to the entrance are nice round ones set in cozy alcoves – no wonder they're already booked. That means, however, that I have to maneuver the narrow path between them, packed with people currently trying to squeeze through as well, plus waiters who are already hurrying to their first patrons.

One look at Romina is enough communication between us. She steps behind me and folds out the controls behind the headrest that allow her to steer the chair. I hate when anyone does that, even her, since the powerchair is the only thing that I have some control over. But I know it's necessary sometimes, for example when I have a bad spasm day and simply can't manage to master the joystick at all or when the situation is complicated enough that it requires someone with better motor skills than mine.

Like right now.

Lauren magically stays at my side even when it gets crowded, and that helps to keep people from bumping into me. I don't know if she does it on purpose but I'm certainly grateful for it. When I'm not controlling my chair I feel powerless enough without people randomly crashing into me, only to look down when they realize they walked into something below their eye level, their faces freezing in shock when they see me. No, I definitely can do without that.

We reach our table without causing too much trouble. It might have also helped that most people were still searching for their tables and didn't pay much attention to their surroundings, so my entrance went unnoticed for the most part. Our seats are at the head of a longer table. The position is very convenient for Romina to assist me and Lauren to sit in front of me at the same time and I inwardly congratulate Romina for what I'm sure was a rather fierce discussion with whoever manages the seating. I smile at Lauren as she hurries forward and removes the third chair, pushing it to the side and closer to the wall.

The two young men right next to us at the table look up when Romina bumps the wheelchair into the table's leg during the process of parking me, our empty wine glasses on the table swaying precariously. Well, no one ever said my aide was perfect.

"Sorry," Romina murmurs to me as she sits down at the head of the table and I give a short snort, knowing she'll understand that I'm not angry with her.

"Good evening." Lauren smiles at everyone while Romina just nods into the round. I do nothing (well, obviously not *nothing* nothing. I guess my legs kick some and my contracted left arm trembles at my side. It wouldn't surprise me if I were drooling a bit). The blond guy diagonally across from me takes a brief look at me, winces and hurriedly lets his gaze move on. The guy to my left remains with his wine glass raised halfway to his lips, forgotten, and stares at me from the side, his eyes bulging considerably.

"Um uh... Good evening..." The blond guy diagonally across from me seems to have concluded that Lauren at least is safe to converse with. "Uh... did you enjoy the conference so far?" he asks her. His smile grows unnervingly wide as he eyes her up and down. He has longer hair, neatly slicked back, and brown tortoiseshell glasses that are probably supposed to make him look intelligent.

I don't think it's working. At all.

"Um... yes, very," Lauren says. "I just listened to an interesting talk from Patrick Hallman here."

That jostles the guy to my left out of his stupor and he finally places his glass down before it can slip out of his hand. "Shit, we missed that, didn't we?" he says to his colleague.

"Was it any good?" The blond asks Lauren, adjusting his glasses pointedly, and leans back, puffing out his – admittedly unfairly broad – chest. "I read a bit of that Hallman guy's stuff." He seems so proud of himself that I wonder if he expects a medal.

Lauren exchanges a quick glance with me and then smirks at the blond guy. "Oh yes?" she asks innocently. "What did you think about it?"

Before he can answer, the guy at my left chimes in. "I never understood much of it, to be honest," he complains in an annoying, nasal voice. He's short but with a broad build, with frizzy, dark brown hair. His shirt sits tight around his neck which makes him look like a clothed chimpanzee. "Too many... indices and mathematical shit and such."

Lauren tilts her head, hiding a grin behind her water glass. "Yes, it can get quite complicated. Ridiculous, really." She lifts her eyebrows at me over the rim of her glass and I suppress a snicker.

This is getting interesting. I rarely ever show myself in public, which is why even people who have read my publications most likely haven't met me in person. And apparently my condition isn't public knowledge, either.

The blond next to Lauren sighs theatrically and rolls his eyes. "Don't pay attention to this guy," he groans, waving a hand at his companion. "My friend here rarely gets anything."

Chimpanzee reacts with disbelief. "As if you understood more!" he protests. "Did you forget throwing Hallman's book against a wall?"

The blond makes a strangled noise and shoots him an angry glance to make him shut up, then he addresses Lauren again. "Anyway... we used the good weather as an excuse to go to the beach today instead. You know...?" He runs a hand over his already behaving hair. "Surfing and chilling a bit. People take this whole thing too seriously anyway." He smirks at Lauren like the bad boy he obviously thinks he is.

Lauren nods vaguely.

"The entire point of this is having fun, isn't it?" The guy continues. With a sigh he leans over to Lauren and places his arm around the back of her chair. Too close, Lauren immediately stiffens, but it's so miniscule he probably didn't notice because he's busy secretly peeking at her décolleté. Suddenly I have this powerful urge to get around the table and punch his stupid glasses off him. Maybe it's a good thing I can't do either. "I'm having fun right now. Are you?" he says, openly leering now.

"Um..." Lauren indeed leans a bit away from him, her nose crinkling in distaste but the blond still doesn't seem to catch the signals. He practically salivates over her.

"Since you've been to the talk..." Chimpanzee tunes in again quickly, apparently afraid to lose ground, "maybe you could fill us in on what we've missed?" There's clearly worry in his voice, too. Probably his boss is going to interrogate him about the contents of the conference and he's afraid for his position. Well, he should be. If I were his boss, he'd not waste my money on the beach again.

The blond nods, his eyes suddenly sparkling as they're still fixed on Lauren. "Yeah, we have time. There sure are things that we can teach you in return... maybe after dinner, though?" He laughs.

Lauren's eyebrows nearly vanish under her hairline. But she's keeping her composure and I can't decide what I find more astonishing: that the two assholes have no idea that their behavior is disgusting or that she hasn't broken the blond's nose just yet. I would have, in her situation. Instead Lauren says: "Well, if you have questions, you can ask Mr. Hallman directly. He's sitting right there."

And then it happens.

Because, believe it or not, the blond guy gets up from his chair and instead of looking at me, the person Lauren is gesturing directly at, he peers over my head to the table behind us, shouting: "Oh my god, really?! Where?"

It's like I'm fucking invisible. Or as if I'm not a person.

Which, for the blond, probably hits the mark.

Lauren looks at me, expression incredulous and her eyes growing larger, and I realize she's nearly bursting with held-back laughter. Although the situation couldn't possibly get any more infuriating for any of us, somehow this girl just makes it all seem incredibly funny.

"Uh..." Alarmed, Chimpanzee watches me, then addresses Romina in a bad stage whisper. "Is he... uh, shouldn't you be doing something? Is he having a seizure or what?"

Romina, my wonderful aide, leans forward a bit, takes one brief look at me and then sits back again, shaking her head shortly. "Everything is alright," she says with an absolutely straight face.

"Oh..." the guy answers stupidly and subtly tries to move his chair further away from me. He doesn't look like he believes Romina and completely fails at disguising a mildly disgusted expression as he watches me. Maybe he's afraid I'm going to puke on him or he'll somehow contract whatever ailment he thinks I

have. "Um... because of... he's... uh..."

"Laughing," Romina says matter-of-factly.

"Excuse me?"

"He's *laughing*," Romina repeats, looking him straight in his face.

"Oh... *Oh!*" Chimpanzee stares at me, wide-eyed. "What is he... what is he laughing about?"

That undoes me. And not only me. Romina and Lauren are shrieking with laughter so loud that people around us jump and crane their heads to look at us. I'm shaking so badly with laughter that my body slides sideways in the wheelchair, despite the support my customized molded seat provides. It takes us a full five minutes during which several flustered waiters walk past our table until we're able to order and Romina gets over it and helps me sit up straight again, wiping tears and spit and whatnot from my face, still giggling. The two dumbheads look confused and indeed a bit jealous at being left out of an obviously great joke and thankfully don't try to rope any of us into conversations anymore.

We choose some kind of peach aperitif wine. It comes in small glasses with a long stem and I put much effort into not choking or emptying the glass in one pull. It works okay and I avoid having to ask Romina to put some of the food thickener powder inside, which always leaves a strange aftertaste. Lauren peeks over at me as Romina holds the straw to my lips and I cringe a bit at first but relax when Lauren smiles her cute smile and downs her glass in one go.

Somehow, we don't exclusively talk about work. Lauren tells me about the struggle of finding an apartment after she moved to her new work place, and about her roommate, an art student with completely reversed working times. They seem to get along well though. Lauren especially likes the cat, although it frequently wakes her up by sitting on her face.

"And that's only the first stage. If I manage to ignore the fact that I have this cat's giant butt in my face and continue sleeping, he will start meowing very loudly into my ear and hit me with his paws. When I get up then, finally, he follows me to the toilet, sits in between my feet and looks at me reproachfully because I dared to empty my bladder before making him breakfast."

I find Lauren's openness irresistible and chuckle at the mental image. "He's probably just preparing you for the time you'll be living with your boyfriend," I joke and we wait for Romina to relay.

I started using the talker at the beginning of our conversation but I soon abandoned it in favor of Romina repeating what I say. It's faster and worth destroying the very vague illusion that we are having a one-on-one conversation here. Plus, whenever I speak, Lauren looks at me as if she's trying to figure out what I say before Romina repeats it and there's a strange, happy glimmer in her eyes. I would almost go as far as to say she may be enjoying listening to my voice, although I honestly don't think that is even possible. Whatever it may be, I find her interest quite endearing and it definitely makes up for the mildly shocked looks that other people throw over to us every time they hear me speak.

"Oh geez…" Lauren says, laughing as well. "Ah yes… I prefer a cat over a boyfriend then." She winks at me.

Does that mean she's single? It's hard to believe, considering she's easily the most beautiful woman in this room. Okay, that's no real feat with hardly any woman present, but you get my point. Does it also mean she wants to stay single or is there a slight chance that I could compete with the cat? I'm not sure who will win, though. I've already accidentally slapped her once, and chances are high it will happen again. So maybe not…?

Romina gives me a short warning signal before wiping spit from the corner of my mouth with a napkin.

Probably not, I guess.

The first course arrives. It's sweet potato soup with pieces of sautéed vegetables and shrimp. For Lauren and Romina it comes in ordinary soup plates, for me in the obligatory high glass into which the soup was poured to further blend it to a completely smooth texture. Romina checks the temperature of the liquid and deems it too hot for me to take up through the straw, so the two women start eating while I wait for my portion to cool down. I'm used to that and it gives me the opportunity to take control over the conversation for once.

I'm curious to know where Lauren is from and it turns out that we're actually from the same region. Since I'm still living only a few streets from the place where I grew up because close proximity to my parents makes my life a hundred times easier, Lauren bombards me with questions of how the rapid growth of the city has changed life there. Apparently, she's thinking of moving back as soon as her current short-term position ends. We argue a bit about the latest city developments but it's more light banter than anything serious.

"I can't believe you were in favor of that insane project," Lauren says, smiling in mild disbelief as she shakes her head.

I try shrugging. "I couldn't have cared less about expanding the airport. But the old one was a nightmare when it came to accessibility, and I knew they had to remedy that during renovation."

"Oh..." It's obvious Lauren has never considered that point and why would she? "Yeah... I guess I see how that makes sense."

The soup has finally cooled down enough and Romina lifts the glass and turns the straw into my direction.

"Does it have shrimp?" I ask her, eying the liquid suspiciously.

Romina shakes her head and rolls her eyes. "Of course it doesn't," she says. She knows I hate everything that comes out of the water. Maybe I wouldn't if I could chew it properly, but at least blended everything fishy just tastes disgusting. It's marginally better with meat, which is why I was endlessly relieved to hear that there was an alternative to the lobster.

The soup goes down well and Romina makes me eat all of it. She has a close eye on my diet and with her watching over it I've actually managed to gain weight during the last year. Which, for me, is a remarkable feat.

The main dish follows shortly after the soup. The lobster is already shelled and I have to admit that it doesn't look so bad.

This can't be said of my steak, however. Even Lauren obviously can't help but lift an eyebrow as the brownish, slightly clumpy puree is served in a deep plate in front of me, and Chimpanzee and the blond guy stare with blatant disgust at it.

"Uh-huh..." I say, smiling somewhat stiffly into the round. "Enjoy your meal, everyone."

Romina tests the temperature and texture of my food and scoops a bit of the mass onto a spoon. I'm trying not to look at anyone, especially not at Lauren, as Romina leads the spoon to my lips and I open my mouth to accept it. Romina is a champion at spoon-feeding me. She knows to wait for the moment when my head doesn't move so much, knows how to smoothly slip the spoon in between my lips without smearing its contents all over my face and the right timing of retracting it again, before anything I still have in my mouth can spill out. With her assistance I eat a few spoonfuls of what tastes remotely meaty and a bit of potatoes, but mostly rather bland with a consistency of mashed up cardboard, stubbornly keeping my eyes on either the plate or the spoon.

"How's your steak?" Lauren asks with a shit-eating grin. "Did you order it medium or rare?"

I nearly spit a mouthful of brown blended mass across the table.

Lauren's grin only widens.

Romina clicks her tongue. "Geez, Patrick..." She's ready with a napkin to save me from the outcome of the accident. "Concentrate."

I do as I'm told and manage to convince my tongue to move most of the rest of what I still have in my mouth back and swallow. "You're the devil," I wheeze after a few pathetic attempts at coughing, glaring at Lauren over the table.

Lauren beams at me innocently. "I was just being polite," she says, playing offended. "It looks formidable."

"Ugh... if you like it so much we can swap," I snap, albeit grinning. God, this girl just manages to turn my mood around like nothing.

"That's very considerate of you. But thanks, I think I'm fine with the lobster," Lauren retorts, beaming, and lifts a piece of rosy meat on her fork to her lips, her large, intense eyes on me.

I blush under her gaze and hurriedly turn back to my meal. The two guys next to us goggle over at us and look as if they've completely lost track of what little brain they possessed.

After the main course there's a short break. The table's discussion moves to politics and I join in whenever I feel it, but mostly I listen. Lauren is talking to the others but she looks at me from time to time, her eyes expressing entire conversations, and I feel content just watching her, taking in everything about her. I love the way she picks up her wine glass, very far down the stem with her fingers, and tips her head back just a little when she drinks, regarding me over the glass, the skin around her eyes crinkling with her smile. Once, a lock of her hair falls forward over her shoulder, and she reaches up and tucks it behind her ear. For a moment I wish her hand was mine and I could do this mundane gesture for her, letting the pads of my fingers glide over her smooth cheek in the process.

Usually I forbid myself thoughts like this because they lead to nothing. I mean, even given the miniscule chance that one day we'd be emotionally close enough that I could be allowed to do this, I'd never be able to physically go through with it.

"What are you thinking?" Lauren asks out of the blue.

I blush upon being caught staring at her and stutter something about what to do the day after tomorrow, once the conference has ended. Not even Romina is able to pick my mushed-together words apart, so I just shake my head.

I can't help but feel a little sad, despite the rather charming dinner. I usually don't tend to feel sorry for myself because I know that despite the shit I'm going through on a regular basis, I'm really rather privileged. I have all the emotional support I could wish for, a caring family and amazing friends, and financially I definitely can't complain. But right in the moment I'm just absolutely crushed by the fact that in two days I'll have to say goodbye to Lauren again, that we didn't have more time together because I'd love to listen to so many more stories of her and the fat cat, or basically every single thing that matters in her life, and that there's no way she'll ever see more in me than a nice guy with a PhD and a wheelchair.

This happens sometimes, sadly enough. People find me interesting, because of the disability or because of my professional achievements. Or both. But that interest evaporates as soon as they start to get an idea of what most of my life really looks like.

And yes, whatever sexual tension I could feel between Lauren and me before has dwindled, which is partly good, I guess, because it made me relax and enjoy dinner with her. It also means, though, that I've lost all hope that this night could end differently than most of my nights. Romina has already sent me a telling look and I know it's about time for me to retreat into my hotel room.

I rest my head back against the headrest and swallow a sigh. Lauren cards a finger through her hair and smiles her wonderful smile when her eyes find mine. She seems to enjoy herself, being here with me. I can't help but smile back at her, a comforting warmth flooding my stomach.

Just like this I realize there's no real reason for me to be in a bad mood after all.

CHAPTER 4

Berating myself for wallowing in self-pity, I dedicate myself to the task of making Lauren laugh a few more times before I have to leave, just because she looks beautiful when she does. She throws her head back, squeezes her eyes shut while her shoulders jump and her uninhibited laughter is loud enough that people turn their heads around to us.

I enjoy the fact that for once I'm not the reason for drawing attention to us. Not everyone looks directly away again, as mesmerized by Lauren as I am.

Shortly before dessert is served I feel Lauren's naked foot brush against my left shin. It takes me by surprise and I startle violently, nearly knocking Romina's wine glass over. Romina tuts and puts it further out of my reach. I blink at Lauren who smiles ruefully back at me and blushes slightly, which leads me to believe that it was really just an accident.

Only then her naked foot settles on my left knee.

My leg goes into mild spasm as a reaction to the touch, the muscles in my thigh quivering slightly and my knee jumping a bit, but Lauren's foot stays. I can feel her toes curl tentatively around my kneecap, like she's mapping out the contours of the trembling bone. The beginning of a hoarse groan sounds in the back of my throat and spasms rattle their way up to my chest.

Lauren places her elbows on the table and studies me, then quickly turns her eyes away again. She clears her throat. "So… Patrick…" she says and her voice wavers only a bit. She picks up her wine glass, her gaze evading mine as she takes a long swig. "You never told me if you're seeing someone."

I emit a strangled cough. All of this is taking a direction I didn't expect anymore.

Lauren's toes move along the lower part of my knee and the fingers of my right hand tighten around the armrest of the chair. The strain makes my arm shake against the sturdy construction, the veins in my hand standing out. At the same time, heat is rushing south at an alarming rate and all I can think of is Lauren's naked foot on my leg, moving further up.

Shit, what is this girl doing to me?

"I told you about the furry companion in my life. So I think it would only be fair if you told me about yours. Furry or not." Lauren's grin is wide and cheeky, her eyes glinting.

"I'm not... I..." I struggle with speech and I notice Lauren is leaning forward a bit as if eager to understand me, her chest heaving under the low cut of her dress. All of a sudden my head is thrown back against the headrest and my tongue momentarily cuts off my air supply, causing me to panic. I choke a little, wheezing against the obstruction in my throat but then, thankfully, I manage to force my head forward again on my own and breathe freely.

I notice Romina relaxes at my side, her hand lowering from where it has rushed to help me. Unfortunately though, Lauren's foot has vanished from my leg almost immediately. She looks at me with large, slightly scared eyes full of apology, and doesn't seem to be interested in carrying this – whatever it was – any further.

God, sometimes I absolutely detest my stupid body.

The shivers stop ruining my speech, but that's only partly a relief. I swallow and manage to pull myself together. I'm a grown adult after all, at least I thought I was. "There're six women in my life," I say without blinking an eye, tracking Lauren's reaction. I sincerely hope she can be distracted.

Lauren slightly lifts her eyebrows, surprised, but the apprehensive look in her eyes doesn't vanish.

"One of them is my mother. She's the best that has ever happened to me, although I should probably say that I happened to her... Anyway, she's awesome. Just to make things clear: she'll always be my number one."

Lauren snorts and her lips move into a weak grin. Finally.

"The second one is Romina. She's my right hand. And my left. And both of my legs. And more often than not my brain."

Romina mildly shakes her head as she relays this and of course can't resist providing details: "Indeed, Patrick never remembers where he saved the latest version of his talks and he seems to think that one pair of pants is enough for a week." She subtly reaches over to clean spit from my lips. "Really, you won't believe he's a genius if you knew him like I do."

I groan in protest and Romina smirks at me. She insists on calling me a genius despite how many times I tell her I don't agree. I'm not stupid, no, but I've been mostly just lucky to get the education that I got, I was at the right places at the right times, and I worked hard to get where I am now.

I turn back to a grinning Lauren and hurriedly continue talking, my cheeks now probably rivaling the color of hers. "Well… anyway, in addition to that I have two very nice persons alternating in helping me out of bed and assisting me with all that morning stuff that less fortunate people need to do on their own and another two who do the same only in reversed order in the evenings."

I'm always open about the amount of help I need, especially since anything else would be a ridiculous lie. Sometimes it seems that people don't think about it at all, however. I don't know how in hell they expect me to change my clothes or brush my teeth when I can't even control my own saliva, but I've had some seriously surprised reactions to mentioning my aides.

I learned it's better to just throw it out there as early as possible.

"Luckily," I add, "None of them are particularly furry." Though they watch me pee. But I don't say that. There's only so much straightforward honesty that one person can take in an evening.

Lauren thankfully doesn't seem to be bothered easily. She hums and looks at me, tracing the rim of her empty wine glass with her fingers, and her gaze is so intense now it makes my heart rate speed up again.

At that moment our waiter arrives. "Strawberry sorbet with wild berries," he announces and places beautiful arrangements of ice and berries in front of the others, and a grayish mass in front of me. Somehow he manages to avoid being struck by my flailing left arm.

I notice Lauren is still watching me. Her foot hasn't returned to my knee and a part of me is grateful for that while the rest is longing for her to touch me again. But even without her doing that, I know I'm doomed. I don't know how Lauren does it, but just looking at her twirling a lock of dark brown hair around her finger is simply torture. Only for some reason absolutely not understandable to me, it seems that there's something going on with Lauren as well. Her breathing has grown a bit irregular and her pupils are so dilated they're almost black.

Romina lifts the straw to my lips but my left arm is behaving so badly, it's making it difficult for me to keep my head still. My aide lets the glass with the dessert sink again with a small sigh and waits for the worst to pass. Interestingly, Lauren stares even more intently as my spasms promptly crank up a notch, thanks to me trying to regain some control over my limbs. Her eyes follow every jerking movement of my body and although this would usually make me feel very uncomfortable, it's not the case now.

And then it dawns on me.

Lauren isn't staring just to satisfy her curiosity, no. If I'm not completely mistaken she's turned on by what she sees. I can see her breath hitch every time my face contorts with a grimace, confirming my thoughts that she may enjoy watching me, even if she's valiantly trying to hide it. For someone as unpracticed with pleasuring women as me, this is more than just an interesting finding.

It's turning my world around.

The only thing is: I still have no clue what exactly makes Lauren go. Is it my face? My body, as hard to believe as it is? Something else? It's difficult though to form a clear thought when a woman is looking at you like Lauren is doing right now, as if she's about to devour me with her eyes.

After a while I manage to lift my trembling right hand with some effort to gesture to Romina, signaling her to try again with the dessert. Promptly, there's a choked noise from across the table, sounding like Lauren hides a moan behind her napkin. I try sitting up a bit, my right hand clutching the armrest, my head bouncing against the headrest. Lauren's eyes meet mine over the straw that Romina tilts in my direction and when I look into Lauren's heated face, warmth flushes my cheeks as well. Holy shit, she's beautiful falling apart like this. I realize in this moment that as much fun as it is to receive pleasure, it's at least equally as satisfying to give pleasure.

If not more.

I smile around the straw through which I haven't yet managed to pull up any food. Lauren sweeps a strand of hair out of her face, her forehead beginning to glisten and her lips parting slowly. As my arousal builds, the spasms come in intensifying waves. Lauren's eyelids flutter at another jerking motion from my arms, and my cock pulses weakly in my pants and releases a drop of precome. Unfortunately for me, the entire left side of my body tightens up at that, and I hiss at the uncomfortable sensation.

Romina places the glass with the dessert back on the table and examines me slightly worriedly, leaning forward to look into my face. "Everything okay?" she whispers.

Probably she has noticed that my body is behaving a bit crazier than what is normal even for me. My left arm is bent, the fist pressed forcefully to my chest and I'm sitting dangerously tilted to one side. My neck is so stiff I don't even manage to nod in answer. Instead I blink at Romina in the hopes that she'll see the plea in my eyes and just ignore my body's weirdness.

"You aren't coming down with something, are you?" Romina mumbles quietly, her brows knotted. "You should maybe get your pump checked." She slips the end of the straw between my lips again, this time holding a napkin under my chin with the other hand to prevent anything from dribbling onto my clothes.

I inwardly thank her for not tying a napkin around my neck in front of everyone in the dining hall and blink again. I'm relieved that my aide is apparently unsuspecting of what is going on between Lauren and me, and obediently attempt to suck the blended ice cream through the straw. Some of it actually makes its way into my stomach instead of opting out over my chin. It tastes relatively good despite the color, a bit like any milkshake you could buy around the corner, and better than the main course by far.

Still, although I put much effort into controlling it, the higher level of muscle tightness brings its challenges. A few times my jaw abruptly clenches down on the straw, and globs of cool liquid ooze down the side of my mouth. It makes me cringe every time it happens but glancing over at Lauren I realize she doesn't seem to mind. Her glazed eyes are still trained on me and her ice cream is melting on her plate, forgotten.

Romina dabs at my lips and chin with the napkin and tucks at the other end of the straw until it slides out from between my teeth. "It isn't smooth enough, is it?" she asks, sighing, and moves the glass, critically watching the liquid swirling around in it. I can see darker spots floating in front of the gray background, the shells of the berries perhaps, and I guess I can feel one of them still sticking to my palate.

"I'm going to ask them to blend it a second time," Romina says resolutely, getting up from the table with my glass in her hand. Her own sorbet is slowly turning into similar mush as my drink. "Okay?"

Between spasms I manage an affirmative groan and then my neck flexes as another series grips my body. A hoarse whimper escapes me before I can stop it.

"You don't have serious breathing problems, do you?" Romina asks quietly so that Lauren can't hear, smooths my hair back and eyes me critically. "And no signs of an upcoming seizure, right?"

I shake my head no at her, slightly mortified, and hope she will just leave and not continue poking around. I haven't had a seizure since I got a device installed in my head and my medication adjusted many years ago. My brain might be a bit under-supplied with oxygen right now but it has zero to do with my condition and everything with that wicked girl sitting across from me.

"Good," Romina says, not quite convinced but at least not that concerned anymore. "Because I'm not sure who'd be paying for flying your dead body home and it'd probably be horribly bureaucratic, so I'd really appreciate you waiting until we're home."

I grimace at her. Yep, I guess my aide has learned her fair share of sarcasm from me. Damn it.

Romina is back to serious again. "We can leave now, if you want?" she says in a low voice.

This is the last thing I want, though.

"I'm good," I manage to groan out between gritted teeth. "Have never been better." In fact, a bad spasm day is rarely worse than this. But then again, I usually don't go out when in this condition.

In retrospect, Lauren's reaction to my sorry attempt at speaking might have tipped Romina off, because Romina stills and glances quizzically over at Lauren who has managed to knock her glass of water over. Lauren grins weakly and apologetically, and Romina gives me a stern look before leaving without further discussion.

"I'm sorry," Lauren whispers over the table, watching Romina go while setting her glass upright again. Thankfully it wasn't full. "I shouldn't have—"

I want to shake my head, which merely causes my legs to start jumping around under the table, the footrest complaining loudly. Lauren swallows thickly and bites her lips again, staring at me. My breath hitches at the sight and warm shivers run down my limbs, making the wheelchair rattle. "It's fine," I gasp, throwing it out there in my own voice for good measure. I won't be able to use the talker anytime soon if I interpret the signs of my body correctly.

"Jesus..." Lauren positively moans when the main part of the attack hits me, making my entire body clench up and convulse. Her eyes flutter closed for a second and her eyebrows dip together. My legs are folding tightly at the knees and trembling violently, and the crooked fingers of my right hand close around the armrest in an attempt to brace myself against the assault from my body. I manage to lift my head to look over at Lauren and for a second I'm distracted by a pearl of sweat running into her décolleté.

Then a violent spasm makes my body jolt and my back arch spectacularly, every single vertebra screaming.

"It's um... warm in here, isn't it?" The blond guy asks Lauren.

Lauren looks at him only fleetingly but she nods, flapping air with her hand into her face. "Oh god yes, so very hot." Her voice has dropped a few pitches, touching something deep within me.

I want Lauren so badly but I know there's nothing she can do for me now. People are sending glances over to us, guiltily watching the weird guy in the wheelchair being ripped apart by spasms. I can feel their eyes on me as the straps around my chest cut deeper into the skin as my upper body rocks forward repeatedly, throwing itself into the restraints. My left arm contracts, pressing against my side, while my right hand is clenched into the armrest. I couldn't let go even if I wanted to. In contrast to normal, though, I lack the shame upon being watched in this state. The skin-crawling feeling that makes me wish I were invisible is completely absent. The thought of Lauren being aroused by it, even if I'm still having a hard time figuring out why that is exactly, is all I care about. I realize that I'd probably let thousands of people watch if Lauren was one of them.

I hear Lauren gasp and her wine glass clink as she places it back on the table, the impact slightly harder than normal.

"Your ice cream..." I force out between painfully clenched teeth, perfectly aware that Lauren probably won't understand a single thing because my speech is beyond comprehensibility. I'm not even sure Romina would manage to make out a word.

Lauren's knuckles turning white around the table's edge tell me that I'm on the right path, though. "It won't... taste better.... when it's melted, believe me." I need to take long breaks between words because my throat is seizing and my chest contracting, and I need most of the air that I manage to inhale for actual breathing.

Lauren leans forward and a shudder goes through her body.

There's a series of terrible grimaces disfiguring my face and making it impossible to even attempt speech. When I regain a fraction of control, I gasp: "It'd be a shame if something as delicious as this dessert should go to waste..." A guttural groan is pumped out of my chest, my throat feeling raw as the sound forces its way through and then it's all suddenly over.

I'm sinking down in my chair with a hoarse sigh, my head lolling forward until my chin rests on my chest, so I can't see Lauren anymore. I can only hear her long gasp. And then she stills in her chair.

One thing's for certain: there's never been a more satisfying sound.

It takes a while for my body to recover from the torture it was put through, my muscles still aching faintly with the memory of the spasm attack. I force myself to breathe steadily through my nose and think of something other than the glorious fantasy of Lauren's fingers on my skin or her hot body against mine, although it's quite difficult. My muscles are too slack for what I experience as normalcy but I manage to plant my right foot more firmly onto the footrest and push up a bit, settling myself as upright as possible on my own, my head falling back against the headrest again. I turn my head with some difficulty and see that Lauren has switched into Romina's seat.

"Drink?" she asks quietly and tips my glass to me. I stopped drinking anything but water long ago; too much alcohol doesn't mix well with either the spasms or my medication.

"Hngh..." I manage a nod and gulp down water as if I'm about to die of thirst, Lauren's fiery eyes burning on me.

"Is he okay?" Chimpanzee asks with a mixture of alarm and

morbid fascination on his face but Lauren silences him with a glare. The blond guy across from us is looking from me to Lauren, incredulous understanding dawning so slowly on his face I almost choke on my drink. I can't stop grinning though.

I turn back to Lauren and want to type something on the screen but my right arm has fallen into the gap between my thigh and the armrest of the wheelchair and it feels much too heavy to pick up right now. My tongue isn't cooperating at all and nothing more than a rattling groan comes out of my mouth.

I can't even thank Lauren, I can't tell her how amazing I think she is, I can't tell her that I've never felt myself falling for anyone so quickly in my life, I can't, I can't—

"Hey..." Lauren says softly, and then she lifts her hand and dabs at my chin with a napkin.

I freeze instantly at the intimate gesture that I hate so much and that condenses all of my worst shortcomings in a painful way but I relax against the strap around my chest when I see her blissed-out smile never fades. There's no pity in her eyes, only warmth.

And the strung-out expression of someone who has had a very good time.

It's all I need to know.

"That was fucking hot, Patrick," she whispers and smiles at me. "Thank you."

Lauren apparently doesn't really care if our seat neighbors hear her, and a comfortable shudder crawls down my spine. All I can do is smile at her with joy and gratitude but I hope it conveys what I'm feeling because in this moment I think I'm the luckiest guy on the planet.

CHAPTER 5

Romina returns after the time it would take to blend every single dessert in the entire dinner hall. She places the glass on the table and comes around to me, businesslike, hooks her arms under my shoulders to pull me upright, tightens the strap over my chest and puts my right hand next to the joystick again, like she does countless times a day. Her face is carefully guarded while she works with me, then, without a word, she sits in Lauren's abandoned seat, looks from me to Lauren and finally moves the glass with the dessert over to me with a questioning quirk of her eyebrows.

I'm so terribly grateful that Romina doesn't speak what I'm almost definitely sure is on her mind that I nod and let Lauren assist me finishing dessert. Under normal circumstances I'd never have allowed it. There are only a few of my friends I feel comfortable enough with letting them feed me and none of them are women I'm emotionally drawn to. Most definitely none of them have just nearly made me orgasm in public.

Or I them.

Well, both were a first, anyway...

Strange enough I end up enjoying it. Lauren's eyes never leave mine as she holds the glass up and the straw in between my lips, moving it quickly with the unpredictable jerks my head does from time to time, preventing the blended ice from spilling. I study her still slightly pink face with the freckles standing out more now, her red lips curved into a small smile, and none of us speak for the entire long time it takes for me to drain the glass.

It doesn't escape my attention that Romina scrutinizes Lauren while she assists me, sitting with her arms crossed, as if waiting for Lauren to make a mistake.

She doesn't. My shirt remains more or less spotless (the champagne from earlier thankfully didn't leave stains) and I don't choke. Lauren is incredible in anticipating my needs, giving me just enough to drink from the dessert as I like before setting the glass back down. I never have to beckon for the next sip because Lauren is already in position.

The rest of the evening is almost over by the time I'm finished. Most people are about to leave when Lauren removes the straw from my lips and places the empty glass on the table and I know it's more than time for Romina and me to head out as well. With that a myriad of thoughts come back that I've ignored successfully until now.

What will happen now? The conference is a big one and we might not necessarily cross paths again. But I don't want it to be over, I realize. Not now. Never, if possible.

I know we're not there, yet, though. Not by a long shot.

That's when I realize I need to propose a second meeting to Lauren. Lauren has seen a lot of me already and to put it lightly: she didn't seem completely taken aback by all of it, right? That's something. Or was it just a one-time adventure for her, a little fun with the guy in the wheelchair? Am I reading more into this than there is, perhaps? And even if Lauren is interested... where will we take this? Could we make this work beyond the conference, with us probably being a couple of flight hours apart? It wouldn't be my first long-distance relationship, for all that's worth.

I know I'm getting ahead of myself. But this is going dizzyingly fast.

Usually I take my time getting to know people, or better, giving people time getting to know me. Most often we start out mailing each other because that's where my forte is: in the written word and long breaks between messages. When that seems promising we meet for short times in neutral places like a park where I can steer the powerchair myself. And only when that works out do we transition to something more intimate, something that places me in a much more vulnerable position, like a dinner.

Never do we jump all these stages and arrive at where we are now within just a few hours. That's insane. And at the same time the most exciting thing that's ever happened to me.

I need to get Lauren's contact data, at least. Maybe we can write each other, which would be the proper thing to do. I want so much more but I need to start with the basics.

By this point I'm so worked up, though, I can't bring myself to ask for Lauren's number or email address in front of Romina. What if Lauren is not interested in seeing me again? What if this was but a nice evening for her, and nothing more? What if I get rejected? At least I want to be rejected when I'm alone, without an audience, even if it's only Romina and I barely have any secrets from her.

I want to have this secret.

When we're just exiting the dining hall and I'm still desperately trying to figure out how to get to speak to Lauren alone, the situation is taken out of my hands.

"I'm thinking about going to an art exhibition the day after tomorrow. In the afternoon, right after the conference ended and before my flight home," Lauren says offhandedly, as if it just occurred to her. "My roommate suggested it. The exhibition is called 'Eat Art' and will be all about food and art. I thought you'd maybe like to join me?"

She looks at me and then at Romina, her hands gripping the strap of her bag.

First I can't believe my luck but then reality crashes in. I'm not sure if we'll have time for that, because although my flight is late in the evening on that day, Romina and I will probably have to be earlier at the airport than Lauren. Getting me into an airplane, along with all the check-ups and the physical process itself, is a never ending story.

I'm about to voice my concern when Romina jumps in. "Why not?" she says to my utter surprise. Usually she's the first to advocate for plenty of time ahead at the airport. Mainly because it rests on her shoulders to get me ready for flying on time. "You two could take a taxi from the hotel, I'll get everything sorted out and we can all meet at the airport."

I stupidly blink at Romina, disbelieving. I've never heard her suggesting I go out on my own with a practical stranger. Romina and I come as a package. Even my closest friends have had to go through an almost year-long vetting process to get that kind of clearance from her.

"Yes, excellent idea," Lauren says, smiling almost shyly at Romina.

Romina's hand trails along the armrest of my wheelchair. "You'll need to know a few things." She stares at Lauren as if attempting to x-ray her.

Lauren straightens under the gaze and nods. "I guess so. If you'll show me..."

Romina remains silent and then, after a while, says: "Sure."

I watch the two women standing opposite to each other, not speaking for a while, and I can't help but feel I'm missing out on the main part of the conversation happening. Then they both turn to look at me in unison and wait for my decision, which catches me wholly unprepared. There's a minute of silence and I'm not even really sure what I should say, overwhelmed by the newfound possibilities and unsuccessful in grasping what has just happened, but when I look at Lauren there's no doubt about what I *want*. Even if it's just a few more hours of it.

My right hand is stiff and uncooperative and Romina and Lauren end up waiting some extended time for me to access the talker. Finally, I manage to convince my knuckle to connect with the field on the screen.

"Okay," says the computer voice.

Lauren beams.

Later I'm lying in bed, freshly showered and naked except for my boxer shorts. By now it's really well into the night but I prefer sticking to my routine.

Romina is rubbing lotion into my skin because it tends to get dry very fast, in every climate. She's wedged a rubber foam pillow under my knees and a smaller one partly under the left side of my back to make lying on my back more comfortable for me. I can't lie stretched out because my muscles will not allow my legs to straighten completely and my spine is crooked from years of gravity and spasms pulling at it in different directions.

"So…" Romina says and takes my left hand into hers. I try relaxing because I know what's coming but I also fear it's pretty fruitless. "That girl…" Romina massages my palm, gently coaxing my fingers to come out of forming a fist. It hurts but it's not unlike anything I've ever experienced. "You like her, huh?"

"Mmmmh…" I try not to give away if I'm confirming or denying her thoughts, evading Romina's inquiring gaze.

Romina slowly pulls at my left hand, her free hand working down along my bent arm at the same time. "You like her a lot even, I'd say."

I can hear the grin in her voice and I know she's enjoying this. My teeth give a squeaking sound as I clench my jaw a bit harder than intended. Sometimes I debate if I should get a new aide, someone who's not as damn curious as Romina. Someone who knows their bounds better. Alas, I'm pretty sure there's no one better than Romina in the entire world and I don't really think about ever replacing her. Only some days I wish she'd be a little less… nosy.

Romina applies lotion onto the skin of my left arm before snatching the brace from the nearby table and putting it on her knees. It will keep my arm somewhat straight during the night, to prevent it from becoming completely immobile one day. Not that it would make a huge difference for me since it barely has any function as it is. But I guess it has something to do with hygiene and being able to clean the crease of my elbow.

Yes, a very appetizing topic, I know. I can tell many of that sort.

"She likes you, too."

My head swivels around to look at Romina so fast I

might've pulled a muscle. Not really, though. I think it would be impossible for me to do that by voluntary movement. Involuntary movement is on another page, however. I literally managed to fracture my shin once while sitting, just by crashing it into the edge of a nearby wall with heavy spasms. My bones are rather brittle though, so that might've played a role as well.

I scowl as Romina grins at me triumphantly. "Come off it," I drawl. "That's not true." Yes, Lauren likes something about me. Doesn't mean she likes *me*. But still...

I haven't been able to stop thinking about that for the last hour. Lauren is definitely into me, somehow. Something about my body, how it moves and my speech, or lack thereof, must be arousing to her. It certainly doesn't make the least bit of sense to me but strangely enough I feel like I don't necessarily need to find sense in it. It's definitely the first time in my life that something like this has happened to me, that I'm able to turn on a woman with just my voice or a gesture of my hand. In fact, if I'm being honest, it's probably the first time in my life that I've been successful in eliciting sexual desire in another person, by my physical appearance alone. I don't really have problems with getting people interested in me, the wheelchair alone does that. And people usually like me, once they get to know me, though I do wonder about that. But I guess it's kind of obvious I struggle with everything coming after that. Apart from trying to keep my body in reign during intercourse there isn't much I can *do*, either before or during or after, and most often I'm not even really successful in doing even that. I must admit it feels amazing, having such power for a change, this gift to make someone enjoy a moment, truly. And I've decided that it feels just too damn good to keep thinking about the reasons behind it.

For now.

But it still doesn't mean that I'm more to Lauren than just some guy.

Romina shrugs. "I tell you," she says. "The way she looked at you... I'd say she is as screwed as you, Patrick."

"Bullshit." The words come out with more force than I wanted to and my whole body jerks violently. Geez, so much for keeping it cool.

Romina clicks her tongue and easily counteracts my weak flailing, not letting go of my arm. She's finished stretching it so that it fits into the brace. The brace is a pretty bulky and ugly construction, with sturdy metal bars keeping it in a locked position and two large flaps that go around my upper and lower arm and can be fastened with Velcro tape. Well, it's only for use during the night and no one except for Romina and my other aides will see it, so I don't care how it looks.

I roll my eyes and huff through my nose. "How long have you known?" I can't keep myself from asking.

"Oh, Patrick." Romina chuckles as she pulls the Velcro securely and shakes her head at me as if I'm a dumb child. Probably I am one, though. "You must think I don't know you at all." She gives the brace a pat when she's finished and smirks. "I hope you hold me in high regard for endlessly bothering the kitchen people about blended ice cream."

I groan. Of course. Romina leaving the table for such a long time was on purpose, to grant me some privacy and to give me time to set me up with Lauren. Well, I can't say it hasn't worked.

Watching Romina grin at me, I love and hate her equal parts I guess.

Romina giggles. "You should've seen the face of the person responsible for desserts in the kitchen when I made a huge show, requiring him to blend the ice cream over and over again. Poor guy."

I can't help but smile.

"She's pretty," Romina says after a while. She's managed to sort my feet and wiggles my shorts up between my clenched legs until they reach my hips. Then she slips my arms through the opening of my sleep shirt and pulls it over my head. She removes the smaller pillow under my back to roll me onto the side. "And your type."

"Mmmmh..." I reply.

"You got to admit to that at least," Romina teases.

"Hungh…" I nod into the pillow, my mouth a bit obstructed by it. Romina flattens it so that I can breathe and pulls my shorts over my ass and the shirt down my back.

"Did you—" Romina starts.

"Romina!" I warn her. This is really none of her business. Of course, I'm sure she has noticed the dried precome in my protective underwear. But talking about it really goes too far.

Romina turns me onto my back again, sighing slightly. "Sorry," she says, but she looks more sorry that she didn't manage to wrangle more out of me, not so much sorry for overstepping professional boundaries. She adjusts the pillow under my knees, secures the ones around me, pulls the light blanket up to my chest and places my arms outside as I prefer it. "Do you need anything else?"

I shake my head.

"Good. Just call me if there's anything." Romina sets up the baby monitor on the bedside table.

Yes, I have a baby monitor.

It means that I can sleep in my own room and don't have to share one with my aides. If you can't appreciate the awesomeness of that you're probably a very lucky person.

"Good night," I tell Romina.

Romina gets up and is about to leave the room when she stops, hand already above the door handle. "Seriously…" she says. "Did she—?"

"Romina!" I can't prevent blushing though as I think back at Lauren's lips parting in pleasure.

Romina gasps and the wide, triumphant grin is obvious in her voice. "Holy shit!" I don't exactly know how much Romina knows about my success with pleasing women in bed, but it must go much deeper than I thought it was. Definitely much deeper than I'd prefer it to be.

I try looking at her but it's hard for me to keep my head up or even remotely sit up without any grab bars installed around the bed. I have them at home, but of course the accessibility of hotel rooms only goes so far. I'm lucky that my electric wheelchair fits through all relevant doors and that there's space next to the bed for the lift we rented. I groan. "Romina, I swear…"

Romina laughs and I can see her waving a hand. "Good night, Patrick. Sweetest of dreams."

If I could I'd throw something at her. But as it is I just glare at the ceiling, hoping she can see it from the door and try my best not to smile.

Because I really do hope for sweet dreams.

CHAPTER 6

I briefly debate imitating the jackasses from the conference dinner and letting the rest of the conference slide to have more time to spend with Lauren the following two days. However, I have a ton of important meetings to attend and discussion rounds I can't miss, and Lauren has appointments, too, she told me. After all, this is still business for us. So we simply exchanged numbers and decided on a time when she'll pick me up at the hotel after the conference has ended.

I'm in the middle of eating breakfast the next morning in my hotel room when there's a knock at the door. Before I can react, the door flies open and Romina sticks her head in.

"Wu wother iffs on fype," she says, her toothbrush still in her mouth and her hands occupied with my laptop. Her curly hair is already tied in a messy bun and she's changed out of her sleeping clothes by now. She isn't a morning person while I usually wake up before the sun, so you'd think we weren't compatible at all. But somehow she's figured out a way to wash and clothe me in the mornings while still halfway asleep and it's working surprisingly well, although I sometimes need to remind her that she has already shampooed my hair and I always keep a close eye on my clothes to prevent them being inside out.

Now, quite some time after I woke up this morning, Romina seems to be awake. As far as I can tell. Even with her toothbrush in her mouth her words are probably ten degrees clearer than mine, but that still doesn't mean I can understand her. It's not like only because my speech is garbage that I can understand everyone else's.

I swallow my breakfast (a shake the color of puke that, as far as I'm informed, is supposed to be a mix of milk, fruits and cereal but that I suspect could really be pieces of my hotel room's wallpaper dissolved in orange juice) and release the straw to turn my head around to Romina. The tip of the straw promptly turns away from me, facing the other way now.

Crap. Of course. It will be a pain in the ass to move it back without knocking the entire glass out of the cup holder by accident.

"Pardon?" I ask Romina, staring hard at the straw as if attempting to make it move by my own force of will. If ever anyone manages that, I'd like to be their apprentice, by the way. It would be enough for me to be able to move straws, forget about anything else, really.

Romina grunts, shifts the laptop to balance it with one hand and removes the toothbrush. "I said, your brother's on skype. Do you want me to—"

"*Just give Patrick to me, Romina. What's so important, anyway?*"

That's my brother's voice. I recognize the perpetually teasing undertone in it, even though it's distorted over the laptop's speakers.

Romina glares at the laptop's screen that I can't see from where I'm sitting in my wheelchair. "Food, William," Romina snaps. "It's kind of important for living. Actually, I'd thought you of all people must know."

My brother laughs raucously and shoots something back that I don't fully understand from the other side of the room. I wiggle my head at Romina. "It's alright. Give him to me. I'll finish later."

Romina sighs and marches up to where I'm sitting at the window with the view over the city. She slams the laptop down on the table in front of me. "You've got five minutes," she says strictly. "We didn't really do any stretching yesterday. And this better be empty when I return." She taps the shake, but it doesn't escape my attention that she quickly moves the straw back to point in my direction before she retreats.

She's an angel. Of the pesky kind.

I groan for show but smile at Romina's back and then at my brother. He's sitting in his office behind his desk and is currently cleaning greasy fingers on a brown paper towel. From the looks of it, he's just had lunch.

"Good morning, brother," William greets me and gives me one of his signature smiles that brings out his dimples. I guess it's the same smile as mine, only it lasts longer than a split second and his face doesn't twitch with spasms afterward. Our eyes are similar, too, as is our hair, thick and of dirty blond color. My brother wears it cut shorter than I do, with only the front getting a bit tousled. Apart from that we couldn't be any more different. For starters, there's no wheelchair on my brother's side of the screen. He slouches in his office chair as much as I do in my chair but his body doesn't show the deformities mine does, his movements are controlled and effortless and his upper arms strong if not muscular but rather soft-fleshed below the rolled-up sleeves of his shirt. There's a bit of a paunch starting to show, too. My brother's taste for junk food and aversion to any physical exertion are finally taking their toll. I guess that was what Romina was referring to just earlier.

"It's always a pleasure to talk to your charming aide," William says with a smirk.

"I can still hear you," Romina shoots at him, her hand on the doorknob.

"That was a compliment!" William shouts from the screen before she can go, grinning.

"You've got food on your tie," Romina snaps and pulls the door closed behind her.

My aide and my brother have a love-hate relationship that is somewhat beyond my understanding. But aside from them bickering constantly I know that they both deeply care about me, and hold some grudging respect for each other.

"Good morning, Will." I watch the screen where William is now trying to get rid of the spot on his tie by dabbing at it with another paper towel. It appears to be a mustard stain or something from his beloved hotdogs. He likes them greasy and dripping.

"So…" William begins, squinting down at his dark green tie

that is only marginally cleaner now. His bruised left hand is still bandaged, a souvenir from an accident a week ago, when he fell trying to climb over a fence to search for a lost minigolf ball. In addition to hurting his hand he managed to sprain his ankle, which happens to be the reason why I'm in this hotel room and he is home, and not the other way around. Going to this conference was his task, originally, since I try to avoid being in public as much as possible. "How did it go yesterday?" William grins at me and I feel my cheeks heat up.

Did Romina tell him about Lauren? I can't quite believe she would but then again... she's got a big mouth and she likes to gossip. Great, I really didn't want that to happen, now William isn't going to let me breathe. It always makes him unbelievably happy when a woman even so much as approaches me and I don't think I can face his nagging questions right now. What am I going to say, anyway? That I met an amazing woman who on top of being ridiculously attractive seems to be into me, too? Yeah, no, this isn't a topic I feel comfortable discussing with my brother. We're close, as much by necessity as by choice, but this is something we've always avoided talking about in too much detail.

"Geez, Patrick, relax... It can't have been that bad, can it?" William moves closer to the screen, the concerned frown barely disguised on his face. I notice with some delay that my right arm has gone rigid, the fingers curling into a painfully tight fist, and my left is erratically shaking in its position at my side. My breathing has gone laborious with my chest squeezing and my feet are drumming on the footrests. Damn my treacherous body. "Your talks are usually great, so..."

Shit. The talk. Of course. William is speaking about the talk I gave at the conference yesterday! I can't believe that it's been only one day that I advanced the slides in the room with the eerily quiet men staring at me. It feels like it was ages ago.

I force a hoarse chuckle through clenched teeth and manage to inhale a wet breath. "No, it... it went well, I think." My jaw is tight, too, and my head is bouncing against the sides of the headrest while I speak, spit flying. I check with my brother before continuing. He usually understands me as effortlessly as my parents or Romina, but there are limits, obviously. "There was a... a s-somewhat nasty guy in the... au-audience but... everything else was okay, I guess." With some effort and several breaks, I manage to tell my brother about the older man in the gray suit who more or less openly doubted my results were real. William watches me attentively and nods from time to time, holding his bandaged hand up when he doesn't understand something to make me repeat, but doesn't interrupt. It takes a while until the spasms subside and by that time I've told almost everything.

"Ah..." William leans back in his office chair finally, nodding his head. "Hebert... Yeah, I know exactly who you're talking about. Sorry, I should've warned you about him. He's a bully. Didn't know he would be at the conference, though. He has been quite successful in his early days, though not so much anymore. That's probably why he's being such a douche in general. And then we aim to replace the method on which he partly built his career with a much simpler, cheaper one... No wonder he's pissed." He laughs. "Well done, dude, at any rate. Guess who will be at the next talk this guy gives, huh?"

I shake my head mildly. "Will..." William has always been quick to defend his pride, and that usually includes me as well. I don't need him to fight my fights, though. We've gone over this a million times, to no avail.

William waves my protest away with his injured hand and pulls a small plastic container toward himself with the other. "Please, let me have some fun, Patrick. You know I get less and less of it these days." He winks at me.

I sigh but I quit my protest. I know my brother too well and there's no point in trying to keep him off something he's set his mind to. Plus, since he's become head of the research department he has been a little stressed out, so this may actually be a welcome distraction for him. I for my part am glad that once my brother's back on his two feet, I can resort to my part-time consultant position, and stay in the background.

William opens the plastic container, sniffs at the contents and pulls out a piece of carrot. He squints at it as if it might physically assault him, then takes a bite off with a suspicious frown on his face.

"What the hell are you eating?" I ask, observing him, and chuckle quietly. I don't know if I've ever seen my brother eat salad. Or any recognizable vegetable.

"Morgan makes me eat these. Says I need to change my diet." William pats his slightly protruding stomach with a sad expression as if it's a departing friend's back.

Morgan is my brother's latest girlfriend. I've met her only on a few occasions but she made a good first impression. She seems to be considerably brighter than the average of my brother's girlfriends, at least. And she didn't stare. Much.

"Not everyone can have your body."

I grimace at William. "Don't think anyone would want to."

William chuckles and tosses back another handful of carrots. "These are disgusting," he mumbles.

"Yeah well..." I sigh, eying the gray, slimy drink in front of me. "That's your point of view, I guess. But haven't you already eaten a hotdog just now?"

William shrugs. "Yeah sure. She said, eat these..." He waves a carrot at me. "She didn't say anything about not eating hotdogs." He looks at me with the twinkle in his eyes that I assume makes the girls swoon. Seriously, when he grins like that he looks like an adorable twelve your old who filched daddy's cigarettes.

I can't suppress a grin myself. As soon as Morgan manages to make him give up eating hotdogs for real, I should probably get a suit tailored for the wedding, I assume. Now that I come to think of it, it occurs to me that Morgan and William have actually been together for quite a while. Much longer than most of William's relationships lasted, if I'm not mistaken. There might really be a chance for wedding bells in the not-so-far future, I'm afraid.

I'm not sure William knows that yet. But I guess he'll be informed soon enough.

"What?" William asks, gesticulating at me with a carrot.

"Nothing," I respond, trying to look inconspicuous. Not an easy task if there's an eternal miscommunication between your brain and your muscles, and sure as shit my face contorts to a grimace. "How is your ankle?" I manage, before my body locks up again.

William's face takes on a theatrical look. That was a good call, my brother loves talking about his various – if completely harmless in the great scheme of things – physical ailments. It will distract him effectively. "Better..." William drawls and sighs. "Doesn't hurt anymore, as long as I don't put weight on it. But it's really annoying not being able to walk properly. And my hand still hurts sometimes."

I don't reply to that. When he told me he couldn't attend the conference to present our research because he didn't want to be stuck alone in a foreign city while being on crutches, and he wanted to send me instead, I tried telling him about the difference between a sprained ankle, and an entirely fucked-up body that needs to be hauled around on wheels, but he barely listened. I don't blame him because I know he doesn't mean it to be offensive. In his eyes, being able-bodied is the norm for him, while for me, it's being disabled. That's just like it always has been and he never questioned it.

Bless him, it must be wonderful to live in a carefree world like that.

I must admit it also fed my ego that he claimed to be helpless with his minor injury, and without hesitation shouldered the responsibility over to me, his brother in a powerchair. Granted, I've got a couple more years of experience in overcoming limitations, but still...

Williams squints at me for few seconds, then he leans back in his chair, weighing his head. "So... Patrick. Want to tell me what *really* happened yesterday?"

Now it's my turn to frown at him. "What do you mean?"

William finishes the last carrots from the bottom of the plastic container and takes a healthy bite with great apparent disgust. "You're not the only genius in the family, brother." He grins triumphantly and sticks a carrot at the screen. "You've got a secret!"

I roll my eyes. "I don't."

"Hah, you never were a good liar. You got all weird before, when I asked you about yesterday."

I snort. "I'm never weird. I don't even know what that is."

William laughs. "Did it happen before the conference talk, or after? Mmmh... after, huh? Don't tell me you actually went to the conference dinner?"

I give him the stink eye.

"Oho! It's something serious. Meaning you didn't meet with a Nobel Prize winner and decided to leave me to work with them, that's a relief. But you met someone. At *dinner*!"

I groan.

"A woman?"

"Okay, geez Will!" My right hand slams down on the armrest. "Yes, it's a woman. Happy?"

William's eyes sparkle. "You bet. What's she like? I hope she's a step up from your usual."

I knock my right hand into my chest, my way of flipping him off. He laughs but waves his hands in defeat. I know he would never have dated any of the women that I've been with, but he knows the reverse is also true.

"Her name is Lauren and she's actually hot," I mumble finally, not looking at him. I don't know why I felt the need to tell him that Lauren is attractive. "Which is entirely beside the point because she's just great," I add quickly.

"Uh huh... she's hot?"

"Yes. And you can shove-"

"Mm..." My brother interrupts. He doesn't seem nearly as surprised as I'd expected. And much less enthusiastic all of a sudden. "How did you meet?"

I reluctantly feed him a few bits of what happened yesterday. "She approached me after my talk. We discussed her research. Then we had dinner." I feel my cheeks warm a bit, thinking about the last part in particular.

William props his chin up on his uninjured hand and seems to mull over that for a while. "What's Romina saying to all that?"

I frown at him. "Since when do you care about Romina's opinion?"

William shrugs, trying and failing at acting casual. "Just asking! Geez." He watches his reflection in the screen and combs his hair back with his fingers. "She probably met her as well. Lauren, was it?"

I snort unconvinced. "Yeah, she..." I think back to Romina's behavior yesterday, her trick with the shake. "I think Romina might like her, actually." It hasn't occurred to me until now but it's true. I'm pretty sure Romina wouldn't have put that much effort into giving us a few minutes on our own if she didn't approve of Lauren.

William leans back from the screen and seems to relax. "Oh well, then. That's... excellent, I guess." He grins. "When is your next date?"

"There isn't—" It's not a date, is it? I'm accompanying Lauren to the museum, nothing else. We all have time after the conference ends and she could have invited anyone, I just happened to be present. Sure, if we had more time to spend together before, get to know each other, a few days working together or something, maybe then our appointment could be called a date. But right now, it's just a meet-up. "I'll see her tomorrow," I mumble.

Will gives me a thumb up. "Go get her, brother!" He winks at me and I groan exaggeratedly.

Weirdly enough though, that's all William has to say on the topic. Not much later Romina interrupts our discussion, announcing I'll be late for my first appointment today, ushers William back to work and watches me like a hawk until I finish breakfast. A short version of the despised stretching exercises follows a hurried brushing of my teeth and then I'm ready to go.

Well... roll.

CHAPTER 7

"Excuse me, young man, is this seat taken?"

I turn my head on the headrest to look at a tiny old man with white tufts of hair standing up in all directions from his oval head and countless lines in his friendly, weathered face. He points to the chair to my right when I don't immediately answer and blinks his clear blue eyes curiously at me as my arm starts jerking upward. "It's just so conveniently close to the exit...," he explains. "Well, and to the restrooms, to be frank," he adds in a lower voice and winks. "Do you mind?"

Slightly taken by surprise, I finally manage to nod my head. Romina accompanied me to the meeting room, which turned out to be a dull seminar room in the basement, with rows of tables and chairs under glaring fluorescent light and a little speaker's desk squeezed on a podium in the front. She moved one of the chairs behind the tables in the front row to the side so that I could park in that spot, and then left to get us coffee. I'm on my own for now. She can sit at my other side once she returns, and no, I don't mind company at all.

The old man smiles and pulls the chair on my right back a bit to sit down carefully, before placing his laptop, his metal coffee mug, a heavy-looking cloth bag with what seems to be several thick paper volumes inside, a notepad, a few pencils and other items on the table in front of us. Then he turns around to me.

"I'm Niels de Jong," he introduces himself and thankfully doesn't try to shake one of my unruly hands. "Although I'm not so very young anymore, I'm afraid." De Jong giggles, the skin of his face crinkling up.

I smile at him involuntarily. De Jong – the young. It's refreshing to meet someone who manages to joke around me.

Most people seem to think it's more appropriate to speak in a fashion they usually reserve for funerals.

I've just convinced my right arm to move halfway back to the talker to introduce myself when Niels de Jong interrupts with a glance at the computer attached to my armrest. "I know exactly who you are, Mr. Hallman. I missed your talk, unfortunately, but I overheard the discussions that flared up after it." He winks at me, again. "I'm glad someone is ready to take on a challenge. No one else seems to have the guts to do that anymore." He laughs to himself as if he's made the greatest joke on earth, his small form trembling on the chair. Then he leans closer to me and says in a lower voice, "And if a certain Theodore gets what is coming to him then I'll heartily congratulate the person who has managed that. And I'm not the only one, mind me. There seems to be a growing group of supporters on your side, who think that Theodore crossed a line during the discussion after your talk, and that he appears to be incapable of accepting that the wind has changed in our field."

A little amused and also alarmed to hear the repercussions of my talk yesterday, but at a loss what to say, my hand jitters, hovering over the talker for a second, but then I thankfully realize I've heard of de Jong before. "I read your book," I type after a while. I remember hearing that at the time it was written, more than twenty years ago, it was very controversial. It has definitely left an impression on me and I furtively sneak a glance at de Jong, the lines in his face, the small tremor of his hands, and notice he's watching me just as closely, no hint of tiredness about him.

De Jong listens to the computer voice with his head cocked, then waves his hand. "It's mostly old men's rambling, now," he says, shrugging.

I jerk my head to the side in a resemblance of a headshake. "I don't think so. It's very... impressive." I mean it.

De Jong beams as if I'm the first to tell him that. "To be honest, we didn't know we were on to something until we were in the middle of it," he says, placing his hands on his chest. "I guess you can call that luck." He sighs, still grinning. "It's not something that people seem to value much anymore. Nowadays it's all about guaranteed results, isn't it? There's no time anymore for intuition, no one appreciates a good guess, don't you agree? And god forbid someone researching what simply interests them!" He mimics being shot in the chest, all flailing limbs and rolling eyes, and I'm not really sure how to react. But de Jong quickly sobers up, sighs, and continues: "A grant proposal is hardly going to be successful if it's not already clear what to expect as the outcome, best if you already have the results ahead of time when you're writing the proposal, am I right?"

I blink slowly, formulating a response using the talker. My head is thrown back against the headrest a few times, disrupting my view of the screen and it takes even longer than usual to finish the sentences. De Jong watches me patiently while I'm typing with a recalcitrant arm, the knuckles of my hand knocking against the screen hard. His curious gaze is quite disconcerting but I appreciate that de Jong isn't pretending he doesn't notice my struggle.

The mechanical voice reads: "I think we need both. Application-oriented research serving a specified purpose. And people looking where no one thought to look before." I watch de Jong for a reaction, hoping I managed to express my thoughts diplomatically enough.

De Jong nods to himself, as if I have confirmed something to him. He hesitates, then clasps his bony hand around my shoulder, making me jump. "Mr. Hallman—" An electronic beep interrupts him and has him turn around to his laptop. "Ah… last minute work, I'm afraid. I should really get this. Do you mind?"

Shaking my head, I smile at his apologetic grin, and leave him to answer a stream of incoming emails before the meeting begins.

While we've been conversing, the room has filled up. People squeezed into the back rows first, but now the seats closer to the front are slowly getting filled up as well. Romina still hasn't arrived back from picking up coffee but I'm not worried. At this time in the morning it may take a while. I choose not to intervene when a group settles into the row where de Jong and I are sitting, and a middle-aged guy occupies the seat to my left without asking if it's free. I don't have plans to participate in this meeting anyway, I'm just here to report news to my brother, if there's anything he doesn't already know. Plus, the guy at my left is furtively looking past me whenever he so much as turns in my direction, and I'm not sure if he'd continue to pretend I don't exist if I attempted to address him directly. I want to spare us both the humiliation of having to interact with each other.

There's a crinkling sound to my right and I notice de Jong has opened one of the paper bags on the table and retrieved a donut to eat while he's working. I can't help but stare at it, my stomach squeezing. Today's breakfast didn't feel particularly nourishing. I'm not really starving, but there is a sudden urge to take a bite off this treat, with the frosting looking sweet and inviting. It's seldom that I feel any appetite at all, so that's quite something.

"Someone looks hungry," de Jong remarks and waves his hand with the donut in front of me. "I have another one if you'd like?"

I shake my head. As delicious as it looks, I probably couldn't eat it anyway. I'd have to take tiny bites, and it would take me forever to finish it. I try to remember if I've ever had puréed donut but I don't think so. It would be a culinary crime, I'm afraid.

Chuckling, I nod with my chin to de Jong. "How did you get one of these?" my computer voice says. I know that officially there's cake and donuts for free in the mornings, along with the coffee, but I've literally only ever seen the remaining crumbs at the buffet. Until now I assumed that's essentially all the caterers put out every morning.

"Oh!" De Jong grins again, obviously happy to be asked, and wipes his mouth with the back of his hand. "Years of experience at wooing the right people." He winks at me. It seems to be something he likes to do frequently. "But if I'm being honest..." He leans toward me and goes on in a lower voice. "The donut shop two blocks down the street makes deliveries to the conference building."

I'm still laughing when I hear Romina's voice from behind me. "Sorry Patrick, the queue was insane." She squeezes between me and de Jong to place a coffee mug with a straw in my cup holder on the right armrest and positions it slightly higher. "Are you alright with me sitting a bit further in the back?"

I nod my head. "I won't walk away," I say sarcastically.

"Good," Romina says and squeezes my arm absentmindedly. Obviously, she isn't nearly as awake as I thought she was.

"Oh, the times when I had a PA," de Jong muses while he watches Romina leave, munching away on his donut. I want to tell him that Romina isn't my PA when I catch him giggling and realize he made a joke.

There's the clicking sound of a microphone turning on and someone clearing their throat over it. "Welcome to today's business meeting." A man has taken to the podium in front of us, older if not quite as old as de Jong, but just as short. I remember him from photos though I've never met him in person. He's the current president of our chapter, Majid Ahmadi. "I'm glad so many have made their way here!" Ahmadi grins into the room that's now brimming with people.

"We are currently adding chairs in the back," Ahmadi goes on. "So everyone should be able to find a seat. Well… can you all see the screen?" There's an affirmative murmur from the crowd, amid the sound of chairs squeaking as people fill the last available seats. Obviously, the committee underestimated the number of people interested in the conference's organizational details. I can't blame them. I have no idea why anyone would be here voluntarily. I wouldn't set a foot – or wheel for that matter – into this meeting if it weren't for William forcing me to be here.

The guy to my left frowns and looks around slightly confused and increasingly alarmed. He probably expected scientific talks in this session and just realized that his way out is blocked. He won't be the only one who mistook 'business meeting' on today's agenda for something more exciting than 'meeting of the organizers of the conference,' and he definitely won't make that mistake again. Believe me, I've been there.

Ahmadi beams "Excellent. Let me begin with a short recap of last year…"

The meeting continues, with statistics and reports of past events, mentions of outstanding papers and awards, and I tune out almost immediately, letting clusters of numbers and graphs slide past in front of my eyes. I'm only present enough to realize that none of what is presented is unexpected or surprising. Some names ring a bell, a few photos spark recognition, but that's about it. Toward the end there's applause to thank the organizing committee, people are called to the front, flowers handed over and hands shaken.

"With that we come to the last point of this meeting, the election of next year's president," Ahmadi says, returning to the podium, in his hands a box of regional baked goods. He places it in front of him on the speaker's desk, where it perches precariously. "I call our nominees to the front, please."

There's a bit of a commotion, as a row behind me people are standing up to let someone squeeze through, while further in the back the same is happening. Three men take the stage, or what serves as it. One of them I recognize immediately: he is wearing the same gray suit, eyes like steel directed at the crowd in front of him. Theodore Hebert, the guy from the discussion after my talk.

"Thank you." Ahmadi grins and nods to the men lining up next to him. "Gentlemen, this is your chance now to convince everyone that you are the right person to replace *me*." He giggles at his own joke.

The speeches are boring. The oldest of the three, a tall man with a curly white mustache and a friendly smile, seems to be only present to make it three candidates. He obviously has no desire to be chapter president and no idea what to do should he get elected by accident. The second guy, a middle-aged, round man with spectacles, tries very hard to make the audience laugh by cracking one joke after the other, but he's clearly not more inspired than the first speaker and people only laugh out of politeness. Hebert's speech basically boils down to maintaining the status quo, though at least he manages to make it sound like it's an awesome idea. Well, I guess things could be worse than that, though I must admit I'm a little disappointed by the lack of enthusiasm.

"Very well, gentleman." Ahmadi rubs his hands. He doesn't seem to be overly surprised; I assume it's not easy to convince anyone to do the job of chapter president. It probably is an assload of work and no real payment. "Now, if there are no additional nominees we'll move on to—"

"Majid!"

Heads turn and I blink surprised because it's de Jong calling from right next to me. He stands up, though even like this he barely stands out of the crowd. He waves his hand a little to get Ahmadi's attention and finally the president spots him.

"Ah... Niels... Did you—"

But Hebert interrupts Ahmadi, putting his hand on the president's arm. "De Jong!" he calls out. "You *do* know that the president's position is required to be held for an entire year, do you?" Hebert has a sickly-sweet smile on his face and leans forward a little as if he is speaking to a child. "Not to sound insensitive but... are you sure you still have that long?" His laugh booms as if he's made a wonderful joke, while the other nominees titter with him, throwing nervous glances at each other.

De Jong doesn't miss a beat. "I've been president more often than I'm afraid you can count, Theodore," he says, kind smile unwavering. "But don't worry, there's no desire from my side to grab the steering wheel again. I wish to leave that to the up and coming and unquestionably more intelligent youth, as we all should, Theodore." He turns a little, waving his hand to the side. "This is why I'd like to propose Patrick Hallman here as nominee for next year's chapter president."

While the people sitting around us fall eerily silent, the rest of the room erupts into subdued noise, chairs rumbling over the floor as some get up to get a better view and others start talking behind their hands to each other, asking what is happening and discussing with each other. It takes me some seconds to realize that I've just been nominated. I stare up at de Jong, blinking furiously and trying to make him turn to me to signal him that I really don't want to become chapter president and that all of this is not a good idea at all. But de Jong doesn't look at me and in fact seems to have entirely forgotten I'm right there.

"Quiet please!" Ahmadi manages to regain control of the room again. His broad smile has vanished, though he doesn't look too bothered by the interruption of business as usual. He watches de Jong, seeming rather amused, if anything. "Niels... proposing another candidate, that's... well within your rights, as you probably know." He sighs, then shrugs. "Well, well. Mr. Hallman, sir..." He turns to me, cringes a little and scratches his bald head. "I assume it's not practical to call you onto the stage. Well... just give your little speech from where you are, if you please, sir."

Oh, this is just going swimmingly.

Ahmadi looks at me expectantly, smiling now.

Where's Romina? No one will understand me if I use my voice, and typing will take for fucking ever. Especially now that hundreds of thoughts are tumbling through my head, all different ways of politely declining, because there's no way I'm actually competing as a candidate, absolutely none. As I'm starting to freak out a little, feeling all eyes on me, the silence ringing louder and louder in my ears with every passing second, my body is going into overdrive. My legs are jerking heavily, making the wheelchair sway and rattle nastily, and my upper body is thrown back against the cushions, audibly knocking my breath out of my chest. My head almost slips from the headrest. There's no hope I'll bring my right hand to cooperate now – it's almost as bad as my left, swinging up and down rhythmically, my fist thumping into the side of the controls. Thankfully the wheelchair's steering system is turned off.

Ahmadi clears his throat. "Take your time. Maybe just start with introducing yourself and then tell us why you'd like to become president."

I know he only wants to help but he has slowed down his speech, enunciating every word clearly, and it's making me furious. It's not the first time I've heard people talk to me like that, even during the last few days. As if I'm mentally disabled as well as physically. I wonder how people think I got to attend this conference, maybe through some quota or out of pity or just as a joke. It doesn't seem to occur to them that I have every right to be here; I am a scientist like them, maybe not as experienced as some, but believe it or not, I didn't get invited as a speaker because of my looks. And I may not be able to speak as well as they do, but god do I understand every single word.

Because it's the only thing that seems left to me, I shake my head repeatedly at Ahmadi and the other people standing in the front. I'm not sure they can recognize it as a shake, amidst the erratic movement of every other part of my body, but I try my best. And one person seems to catch on.

"Now…" Hebert sneers down at me with a predatory gleam in those formerly dead eyes. "I'm not surprised that Mr. Hallman doesn't seem to be very fond of the idea of competing in this election. And he would be well advised not to. Chapter presidency requires a certain level of proficiency and experience that not everyone exhibits. Moreover, considering Mr. Hallman's physical condition, no one will be surprised if he declines the honor. One should even wonder if his physical state will allow him to hold such a responsible position."

As he says this, he looks right into my eyes, his lips pulling into a cruel smile. "Anyway, health should always be more important than power, shouldn't it, Mr. Hallman? We certainly don't want to see you decline even further." While he speaks, a few heads in the audience nod thoughtfully, and the guy at my left side moves his chair even further away from me, as if he is afraid that I'm contagious.

For a moment, fury makes me speechless, even more so than normally. My right hand is forming a shivering fist, the knuckles white. I'm not known to be quick-tempered, but in this moment there's not a single person in the world that I hate more passionately than Theodore Hebert. I can hear my heart thrumming in my chest as I stare up at him on stage, my blood boiling when I watch his triumphant smile widen as he nods thoughtfully, as if he's doing me a favor. I can't do anything to stop him. Even if I managed to access the talker now, typing what I'd like to say would take much longer than anyone in this room has the patience for.

"Patrick."

It's Romina! She's somewhere behind me, clearly out of breath, probably from forcing her way through to the front, but I was never happier to know her with me.

"Shoot," she whispers.

I could kiss her.

"President Ahmadi, dear audience," I begin, and there's the silence again. Hell yeah, having an outstandingly ugly voice has its perks. The spasm attack has almost abated, but my voice is still even more pressed than usual, words even less recognizable than when I'm comfortable. But Romina doesn't miss a beat; she translates what I say in her clear voice that easily carries through the entire room, and if you didn't know her as well as I do you wouldn't notice the little tremble in it, barely audible. Just a hint of it, but it's there. I notice it's probably her first time speaking in front of such a large audience.

"First of all, I would like to thank Mr. de Jong here for the nomination. It is a great honor for me to be considered for this election." De Jong beams at me and pats me on my still slightly quivering right arm. I nod at him before continuing. "As for the question Mr. Hebert raised about my health..." I turn my attention back to the stage. "I can assure you that I have never been healthier than I am right now, and that I would be well equipped to shoulder such a responsibility. But I thank you for your sincere concern, Mr. Hebert."

Hebert looks down at me, the smile still plastered on his face but now it looks more rigid. I have to suppress a laugh and accidentally choke a little on saliva. It takes a few seconds for me to cough it up, thankfully without Romina's help. By then, the room that has started buzzing with whispers has fallen quiet again, everyone staring at me in slight horror. Well, not my best display of perfect health, but so be it.

"This is why," I continue wheezing after a while, "I am very happy to accept the nomination to stand for chapter president." No one laughs at my little joke, but I don't blame them. It takes people a while to laugh about my situation, even if I make the jokes myself. I can hear Romina fidgeting behind me. She didn't believe my talk would take this turn, either. To be honest, prior to Hebert's interruption I had been determined to get out of this nomination by any means. Now there's no such thought left in me, even if it's just to spite the git. I lift my head up to look at a stone-faced Hebert and a gently smiling Ahmadi in front, waiting.

I'll have to come up with a few ideas, at least. Luckily, my previous discussion with de Jong pops back into my head. "As president of this chapter, my main goal will be to support young researchers who lack significant funding, to help them in further pursuing their own ideas and establishing themselves in their field of research. For this purpose I will initiate a challenge among all young researchers, to pitch ideas to a committee that will not only award funding for the best projects, but also mentor the selected researchers and help them build their networks. Furthermore, among all other researchers I will solicit seed money to fund a scholarship for a high-risk project in an underfunded area of research, to find the hidden gems."

I'm dizzy and out of breath after my monologue, even though it was interspersed with several breaks when I had to concentrate on breathing, swallowing or just giving Romina time to relay. My body has calmed down by now, the muscles in my legs are painfully rigid but at least the kicking has stopped. My left arm is only mildly jerking, not as dangerously as before, when the person sitting to my left had to duck a few times to avoid being hit. De Jong nods at me approvingly, grinning like a Cheshire cat. Hebert looks sour, Ahmadi quite satisfied. The room is bustling with talk and Ahmadi has to call for silence twice before he's heard. Luckily for me there are no questions, because I don't have the damnedest idea where the money for the intended funding is supposed to come from, but I guess we can always cancel a bunch of people's business flight privileges or cut down on expenses for dinner meetings.

Right?

"I would like to call everyone's vote now. Please write the name of the next chapter president on the provided piece of paper..." There are small, rectangular pieces of paper placed on every table, but no pens. People scramble to borrow pens from their neighbors and start talking again, until Ahmadi knocks his gift basket onto the wooden speaker's desk and yells at everyone to shut up. I hope there's nothing breakable among his presents. De Jong gives me one of his various pens and Romina writes my name on my paper. I scowl at her because I would rather abstain than vote for myself, and I'm pretty sure she knows that perfectly well. But she ignores me and throws it into the basket that is handed around.

It takes quite a while until everyone's votes are counted. De Jong and I are soon deep in conversation again. Now that Romina is there it is even easier than before. It doesn't surprise me to hear that de Jong and my brother are well acquainted; I even begin to suspect they are both behind my nomination. Well, in any case, I didn't compete because of them.

As de Jong laughs about one of his own jokes, a small sound indicates that I've received a text message. With a shivering knuckle on the screen of my talker I bring it up, reading quickly. It's a text from Lauren. She writes: 'Going to meet with colleagues for lunch today. Care to join us?' Then, after a few seconds: 'Since Romina told me I should get some experience...'

I'm convinced Romina sitting next to me has read the message, too, but she has the decency to act like she didn't. I don't get around to answer Lauren, or think about her invitation, because Ahmadi stands up, indicating the results of the election are to be announced. As I turn my screen blank again, my eyes wander back to Hebert who is still standing idle on stage with the other nominees. His face has returned to its old state, cold and rigid, and he watches the audience with bitter suspicion around his lips, as if he's trying to identify who didn't vote for him.

Well, to cut things short, I don't get elected as chapter president. Not very surprisingly, to be honest, since I'm still pretty new to the community.

The majority of votes go to Theodore Hebert, who manages to look a little less gloomy by the end of the announcement. However, to my own horror, I become vice president, with a noticeable gap to the other two nominees. Which means that Hebert and I will have loads of time to sort out our differences in the future.

Perfect. Just perfect.

De Jong congratulates me effusively, clapping my shoulder and grabbing my hand. "Well done," he cheers in his thin voice. "I knew you could do it." Then he whispers into my ear: "Next time you'll beat him."

Hebert's eyes meet mine and by the hardening glance in them I can see we won't have an easy time together. Considering the number of votes I received today, his animosity toward me probably has increased even more. I understand now that he truly is just afraid of being upstaged by me, shaking limbs and giant wheelchair notwithstanding, and the thought makes me grin a little with satisfaction. At this, Hebert turns away abruptly and leaves the room, with a bunch of loyal people trailing behind him.

In my mind, I can see my brother and de Jong shaking hands and congratulating themselves. This could hardly have been a better outcome for them, and it wasn't even their own doing, at least not entirely. Not even my genius brother could have orchestrated things so perfectly, because if anything can make me do what I'd rather not, it's someone suggesting I'm not capable of doing it.

CHAPTER 8

I'm debating internally while we ride the elevator up from the basement, because Lauren's surprise invitation is something to chew on for me. I'd love to see Lauren, of course I would, in fact I'm thrilled by the prospect of seeing her again so soon. But I need to have more information first. Is the place accessible, for starters? Are her colleagues okay with slowing their conversation down for me, or am I just going to be sitting around, listening to them chat away? Do they know I've been invited at all, and the specifics of that? Inquiring all of this takes much too long to type and I don't want to involve Romina any more than she needs to be. I make sure I have no other appointments around lunch and then send Lauren a quick text:

'Sure. Where?'

This way, I can ask Romina to call ahead and inquire about accessibility. Though accessibility as stated by the owner of a venue and actual accessibility for a powerchair user are two very different things. Usually, I ask one of my aides to check out new places before we go, or follow recommendations of my closest friends or family members who are familiar with my requirements. This time I'll just have to cross my fingers that the information we get is sufficient.

Yep, voluntarily crossing my fingers, that's a figure of speech.

Before the lunch break however, I have to suffer through a few presentations and a podium discussion that would probably have been interesting had not my thoughts been entirely somewhere else. I can't seem to concentrate on the slides or speakers, my mind occupied with Lauren. She's nothing like any woman I have ever met. She's smart and funny, and beautiful, yes, but more importantly, although she definitely notices my disability – doesn't even shy away from the reality of it as many people tend to – I feel like an ordinary man when I'm with her. Usually, it takes a long time for that to happen with people I meet, and with some I simply never forget the differences between us. I'm excited to meet Lauren again, in fact a little nervous, but definitely looking forward to it, and I realize I'm ready to tackle whatever obstacles may present itself at the restaurant.

I'm not usually this adventurous. I like my routines, I like knowing exactly what is going to happen, and I prefer places and people I'm familiar with. My job does require tons of travelling and meeting new people, if I can't avoid it or have my brother do it for me, but I have my routines for that as well and I take my time to plan ahead and prepare everyone.

I don't have that time now. I realize that if I want a chance at getting to know Lauren better before we part, I need to jump into cold waters and meet her colleagues at a place that's completely foreign to me.

Giving up on following a heated discussion about some technical details involving national lab regulations I send Lauren another text:

'Can't wait till lunch time.'

I know Lauren is attending a parallel session, in a lecture hall on the other side of the building. But she seems just as easily distracted as I currently am, because less than a minute passes before she sends a reply:

'You and every other normal person in this building.'

I grin to myself because she's right and because I'm probably not normal in that regard. I usually wouldn't watch the seconds tick by as feverishly as I do now. While I don't particularly enjoy giving conference talks, I actually like sitting in on them, most of the time. When the speaker is good enough, I forget the glances I receive from the people sitting around me, and if I'm really lucky the lecture hall is big and the lights dimmed, and my presence can go almost unnoticed. If I have questions, I usually pose them via email afterward.

Finally, after what seems like endless hours spent waiting and wishing for time to pass faster, the last speaker leaves the stage, and the chairman thanks the audience. Most people have already risen from their seats and are filing out of the hall, hungry and eager to grab a seat in a nearby restaurant.

Romina yawns as she rises from her seat next to me, fanning herself with a print-out of today's agenda, and gives me a pained look. Right. If this is boring for me, it must be excruciating for her. "Let's go," I mumble, the wheelchair jumping forward as my hand accidentally knocks into the joystick a little harder than intended. Romina pulls an empty chair out of my way before I can hit it square, and I manage to regain some control over the powerchair. We make it out of the hall behind the rest of the crowd, slowly but without more incidents.

The air outside is hot and humid, and thick with car exhaust and salt from the nearby shore. People on their way to lunch destinations try to navigate the narrow line between walking slowly enough to prevent breaking a sweat in their suits, and quickly enough to shorten the time until they can shelter inside an air-conditioned building. Romina doesn't seem to be bothered by the heat. She has her eyes on the navigation app on her phone. I'm concentrating on steering the wheelchair, which doesn't go faster than what seems snail speed anyway, while I'm urging it on internally despite knowing it's futile.

We cross the busy street in front of the main conference building, slowly follow its curve down, wait forever at a crossing and move two blocks down another street. By now, the sidewalk isn't as crowded anymore because people have dispersed and also because we are running late. At an inconspicuous corner Romina pauses, consults the navigation app on her phone once more, mumbles something to herself and walks around the corner. I'm about to ask her if we are lost when we find ourselves in front of a door that Romina pulls open, and I steer the wheelchair into a rather small restaurant.

I spot Lauren immediately. She has stood up from her chair in the back of the room and waves at us, which seems a little unnecessary but makes me laugh. It's easy to spot her since the public space of the restaurant consists of just a few tables and chairs crammed into one room. Lauren is wearing a black blouse and a brightly colored skirt, and her hair is braided, a loose strand curling over her shoulder. She enthusiastically continues waving at me, and it makes my smile linger even though I really want to be mad because one glance confirmed my worry. There's no way I'll make it through the tight space to Lauren's table without at least two other tables being moved to the sides, including the chairs around them and people sitting on them. The small restaurant is packed and lunch is already served.

"I'm sorry," Romina says, squeezing my shoulder and somehow that makes the dejection sink in. Why can't anything just be simple for once, as it is for everyone else?

Fuck.

Lauren appears in front of me, slightly out of breath and still grinning joyfully. "Hi Patrick! Follow me!"

She doesn't even give me a chance to greet her, or to tell her that this is hopeless and I should rather just go and have lunch in my hotel, but instead she walks past us and through the door we just came in. Romina turns to me with an eyebrow raised. I shrug and knock a fist into the joystick to make the wheelchair turn on the spot.

We follow Lauren outside who walks down the side of the building to another door. It seems to be the entrance to some nameless company, and she waves through the glass at the person behind the desk until the door is buzzed open for us.

"The restaurant shares restrooms with the offices here," Lauren explains as she leads us past the sleek white desk. She thanks the guy behind it who winks at her, and then heads down a corridor. An automatic door opens slowly, and from the sounds and smells behind it I immediately recognize we are back in the restaurant. This time, on the other side of it.

"We had lunch here last time when we were in the city," Lauren says. "So I knew this is the best way to get you to our table." With this, Lauren rounds a corner and gesticulates to a table just ahead of us, in the back of the small room that we had left just moments ago. Two young women are already seated at the table and are eyeing me curiously. I assume they are Lauren's colleagues.

I'm literally speechless for a moment, and this time it's not spasms that keep me from talking. Romina grins and I finally manage to get a grip on myself and use the talker. "Excellent," the computer voice says and I smile. I can't quite believe Lauren has been this thoughtful and inventive to get me to join her for lunch. "Thanks, Lauren."

Lauren beams at me and almost vibrates with happiness.

I make an effort to rip my eyes away from her. "Let's go, I'm hungry," the reader announces truthfully, and I steer toward our table. But halfway to it, the wheelchair jerks to an abrupt halt.

I stare at the room like I'm seeing it for the first time. And maybe that's right because I had been distracted by so many things. My fear of inaccessibility. Lauren. But now that I have had the opportunity to look at the restaurant a bit more closely, it dawns on me.

"Lauren..."

This truly can't be right.

Lauren stops as well, turning to me at the sound of me speaking. "I know, Patrick, but..."

Someone must have made a mistake. "Lauren, this..." Again, I struggle with words. If I'm not completely mistaken, this place is worse than anything I could have imagined. And I've been stranded in front of stairs that must have appeared out of nowhere because everyone I was with agreed that the entrance was level last time they visited the place without me.

Romina frowns at me and doesn't relay what I said, or better, am still struggling to say. Can't she see where we are? This is...

"A sushi bar," Lauren mumbles, sheepishly, though the corners of her lips twitch. "We booked the table weeks ago. Everything else is full, I checked."

"Oh!" Romina's eyes widen and she looks around, then bursts into laughter. Giggling, she stumbles into the powerchair, bracing herself against the armrest with one hand, and doesn't stop when I glare at her.

How is this funny?

My eyes wander through the small room. There's a small open kitchen in the back, opposite the entrance, and a guy with a white chef's hat is currently cutting a gigantic fish – its head still attached, tiny black eyes glinting at me – into smaller portions while other chefs are manipulating crisp white rice, fish and various colorful ingredients to form long rolls or are busy building elaborate arrangements of raw fish on little plates. A couple of customers are sitting on high bar stools adjacent to the open kitchen, others around the small tables, and literally everyone in the restaurant who has been served food is eating some variation of sushi. There's fish and seafood wherever I look. I doubt there's anything on the menu that hasn't spent a significant duration of lifetime below sea level.

"Don't worry, Patrick" Lauren says. "I ordered for the two of us."

That does *not* succeed in making me feel any better, though.

"What...?" I start asking as I finally follow Lauren to the table, ignoring her colleagues who stare at me a little slack-jawed upon hearing my voice. That's the least of my concern right now. "What did you order?"

Lauren needs a second to parse what I just said because Romina is still hiccupping somewhere behind me and is of absolutely no use to me currently. Finally, Lauren sits on a chair next to her colleagues and crosses her legs. "It's a surprise," she answers and grins. "It wouldn't be fun if I told you, would it?"

A surprise? Fun?

I look at Romina in bewilderment but there's no help to expect from her side. She has taken to sit on the only remaining chair, still wheezing, her eyes glistening with tears from laughter.

I park as close to the little table as possible without bumping into it with the armrests of the powerchair, but I'm still a good distance from it. It will do, though, it's not exactly the first time this has happened. It's a good thing I can't eat on my own, because I definitely couldn't reach the table like this.

"Um..." That's one of Lauren's colleagues. She sports a head of curly blond hair and wears a checkered button-up with rolled-up sleeves. "Hi!" She holds up her hand and waves at me and my aide, smiling bravely.

"Oh!" Lauren remembers and gestures at her colleagues. "This is Paige. And this is Lucetta. Lu, Paige, meet Patrick and Romina."

Time to pull myself together. I can't make a scene in front of Lauren's colleagues. Anyway, it's only fish, I will survive. Or so I hope.

Lu wears glasses and has dark long hair that falls around her face like a curtain. She blinks and seems otherwise too shocked to react. Romina says hi and I try to give my best smile.

Lauren is apparently unaware of her colleagues' uneasiness. She leans back in her chair, relaxed. "Patrick, we were just discussing how to best respond to an email in all caps."

Lu clears her throat and looks at Page, both seemingly relieved they don't immediately have to engage with me. They jump back into the conversation they had before I arrived. "Call them and yell at them," Paige suggests in a distinct Australian accent, and jabs a finger into the table. "Since it seems to be their preferred way of communication."

"At the least reply in all caps," Lu says, fiddling with a package of salt on the table. "Or simply write: 'Your shift key appears to be stuck,' and nothing else."

Lauren points at Lu. "Oh, that's a good one," she says, nodding.

"Who writes to you in all caps?" I ask, curiosity getting the better of me. To be fair, I actually said: "Who... caps?" because I'm lazy and I know Romina will be able to fill in the missing parts.

The sound of my voice causes Lauren's colleagues to flinch and they both turn to stare at me. Did they forget for a second that I was here? Romina relays swiftly and as I intended. While she speaks, Lu and Paige look back and forth between me and Romina, clearly puzzled at first, but after a while, comprehension is dawning. I usually don't explain the presence of my aides. People figure out pretty soon why they are there.

"Oh," Lauren makes a dismissive hand gesture and laughs. "Not to me. To my boss."

I raise an eyebrow, wordlessly inquiring for more information.

"A student who asked about office hours or something. I don't really know, the email was rather confusing, on top of being in all caps." Lauren lifts her hands and lets them fall down again. "My boss forwarded the mail to me, so I guess it's now my job to deal with it."

"Classic," Lu mumbles and shakes her head.

Lauren shrugs. "Yeah, unfortunately I can't ignore it."

"No form of address or anything, I assume?" I ask.

"Nope, that would be way too much to expect, wouldn't it? Reading some of the emails I receive from students, I get the impression my name is 'Yo' or 'Sup'," Lauren says.

"Or: 'Dude'," Paige supplies and shakes her head, her curls flying.

They share a round of laughter. I feel pleasantly reminded of the time I was working as a teaching assistant at university, not so long ago. Although I still sometimes receive emails that lack all form, at least no one goes so far as to call me 'Dude' now. Except my brother, of course.

"Yes, exactly!" Lauren groans. "Some emails are absolutely riddled with typos or mistakes in grammar. Not even to speak of punctuation, which is just completely nonexistent." She sighs. "And most aren't signed."

"Just imagine students would have a look at the syllabus before writing emails to us, because office hours are *in there*," Paige says. "Along with almost everything else any student has ever asked at the beginning of term."

"True," Lu agrees. "But so many people would be out of their jobs if students started thinking on their own."

Everyone laughs, and on the tables around us people turn to look at us, drawn in by the ugly sound of my laughter that lifts above the cacophony of the little restaurant. Lu's eyes meet mine for a split second before she blushes and quickly looks away.

"Reply with a formal correction of their email," I suggest once we've sobered up. Everyone looks at me, blankly, and I hurry to go on. But despite my best effort, it takes a while for me to formulate the words, and this time I don't dare to leave anything out and for Romina to guess at. I don't fail to notice how Lu and Paige seem to get hypnotized by my flailing left arm while I talk. Speaking is an obvious effort for me, so I kind of understand why Lauren's colleagues feel uncomfortable.

Finally, Romina relays: "You know, point out mistakes in red, suggest changes, and post a link to the syllabus and a dictionary, if necessary. Treat it like grading a paper."

"Yeeah," Paige says slowly once Romina has finished, turning from my aide to me again. "That's cool." She nods appreciatively and Lu smiles at me, this time not looking away as our eyes meet, at least not right away.

Lauren grins at me. "You know what? I may actually do that," she says.

Romina excuses herself to order some food for herself at the kitchen counter because all of the waiters seem busy delivering food to other tables and haven't paid attention to our arrival. While she's gone, Lauren and her friends chat about their colleagues and professors at the university they work at, and I'm completely fine with just listening for a moment. Paige does a hilarious impression of their boss, who she portrays as a chaotic and sometimes choleric man, though they all seem to admire him. I don't know their boss, but it's too funny not to laugh when Paige mimics him throwing a fit as he discovered unusually high demands of ethanol in his lab.

"Well, he was right to be angry, most students were dousing everything in ethanol, just to be faster done with the cleaning," Lu points out.

"Sure, but he didn't have to throw a container of it across the lab to prove his point," Paige retorts, throwing her hands up. "He almost hit a student!"

"Imagine the paperwork..." Lu says, shuddering. "Not to

speak of the angry calls from parents."

Lauren looks at me and smiles. This time I don't feel embarrassed getting caught staring at her. I could watch Lauren for hours, as she curls the strand of hair that escaped her braid around her finger, or laughs at a joke, loudly, with her whole body engaged. Her colleagues seem great, and I'm impressed at how quickly they got over the shock of having me at their table. But Lauren takes my breath away whenever our eyes meet and she smiles at me, and me alone.

"Dinner yesterday was pretty good, wasn't it?" Paige says. "I was surprised the conference splurged on lobster."

"Yeah," Lu affirms. "That was very unusual. Also I heard that we'll get to vote where the conference will take place next year."

It's true, it was just announced at the business meeting today. News travels fast apparently.

"Oh, imagine we could vote for Hawaii! Or Mauritius!"

"I sure hope not. That's way too expensive," Lauren mumbles.

"It could be Australia!" Paige speculates hopefully. "That would be a change."

"But, isn't the conference in Europe every second year?" Lu muses.

"That's right," I say.

Everyone turns to me. Ah yes, Romina is still talking to one of the chefs in the kitchen. I wonder what's so complicated about ordering sushi. I suppress a sigh and painstakingly convince my right hand to hit the screen of my talker, which lights up the moment I touch it. But before I can type anything, Lauren ventures a guess.

"Lu is right?"

I try to nod, my head slipping a little to the side on the headrest as a result.

Nevertheless, Lauren beams, obviously pleased she understood me. "What are the options they'll give us?"

"France or Austria." The first one was easy, the second…

"Um… France and?"

I attempt repeating what I just said, but it ends up getting swallowed as my legs decide to ramp up the kicking. Luckily, between the three of them, they rattle through the European countries quickly, and none of the women appears bothered by the guessing game. If anything, it seems to excite them. They go on trying to wiggle the cities out of me, but my head is craned back by a few nasty spasms and I don't get out more than a whisper, my throat tight. It's no use to them. Although they stare at me in single-minded concentration, no one even notices me confirming Paige's guess at Vienna. And I can't access the talker when I don't see it.

"Sorry, Patrick, they have sooo much to choose from. I had never heard of half of the fish they serve here." Romina slips into her chair next to me.

I roll my eyes at her as she turns to me to remove saliva from the corners of my lips, but I can't really make myself be angry at her. Romina looks happy like a kid in a sweets shop.

With Romina's help I explain that the conference next year will be either in Vienna or Saint-Malo, which has everyone very excited, and then our food arrives. Lu and Paige ordered what looks to me like ordinary sushi. Romina has sushi, too, but also the most disgusting fried crab I've ever seen. It seems like it has too many legs, or maybe they are some kind of antennae I couldn't care less. Every part of the animal is slightly covered in crispy fried dough, and Romina announces that even the eyes are edible. Before my stomach can turn itself over, two large glasses with straws are placed in front of me and Lauren, who watches me cheekily.

"What's that?" I ask, eyeing the gray liquid in my glass critically. So far, it doesn't smell of fish, and doesn't look too disgusting, though that's compared to Romina's crab. But right now I don't trust Lauren as far as I can spit. Which isn't much farther than to my chin.

"This is the banana chocolate and peanut butter flavored 37:30:30:3 Phyto-Power shake," the waiter explains to us, trying to avoid staring by not looking at me at all. "With fine powdered tapioca, MCTs from flaxseeds, complete proteins, and phytonutrient polyphenols,"

"37:30:30:3?" My swirling brain clings to the numbers like a safety boat. Phytonutrient polyphenols? Here I was thinking I was on a break from work.

"It's the ratio of carbohydrate, fat, protein and fiber," the waiter explains once Romina repeats what I have said. He looks at me as if that much was obvious, then his gaze lands on my flailing left arm, and he flinches and looks away again.

"Ah. So…" I frown at Lauren. "It's a nutrition shake?"

"Our shakes meet the requirements for all macro- and micronutrients and are a sustained source of energy with a wealth of other nutritious benefits, like antioxidant effects as in our Phyto-Power shake here," the waiter answers in a dizzying speed before Lauren can. He turns to me. "Yes, a nutrition shake, if you'd like to call it that." He wrinkles his nose and I can't help but feel I have offended him somehow. "Any more questions?"

I manage to shake my head and we all hold our breath until the waiter has disappeared. Paige and Lu giggle into their hands and Lauren disappears under the table, laughing hard. She wipes her eyes when she returns back to us. "Sorry, Patrick, that was too hilarious," she hiccoughs. "They take pride in their shakes here."

"Yeah, although virtually no one orders them anymore. But they were big a few years ago," Paige says.

I remember that time very well. In fact, I used to drink a lot of those meal replacement shakes, because they go down much easier than pureed food, and they usually don't taste too terrible. But after a while my doctors insisted I stick to real food whenever possible, mostly to keep training the entire system that is responsible for chewing and swallowing, and god knows I can use all the training I can get in that area. But occasionally I still drink a nutrition shake, when I'm sick or whoever is there to help me doesn't have the time (or skill…) to spoon-feed me.

"Lu ordered a chocolate shake for dessert last time we ate here. We almost got thrown out. Remember?" Paige asks, elbowing Lu.

Lu groans. "Oh right."

Everyone laughs and we turn to our food. Romina moves the straw in my direction before doing unspeakable things to the crab on her plate.

"Is my order okay?" Lauren asks in a low voice that's only meant to be heard by me. She places her hand over mine on the armrest of the wheelchair, her thumb slowly trailing over my clenching knuckles. Lauren is one of the very few people who don't seem to be afraid to get close to me, despite only knowing me for a very short time. For a moment I forget to answer, and just stare at her. As she leans over, I can smell her perfume and notice the golden shimmer in her dark hair, and I forget we are not alone. If I could I'd reach out with my hand and pull her into a kiss. She would get up from her chair and move over to straddle me, her skirt hiking up over her strong thighs and her breath quickening, and she would hold my face with both her hands, steadying my head as her tongue tickles the roof of my mouth, demandingly.

I nod.

Lauren smiles, squeezes my hand and turns to the table, lifting her glass to the group. "Today we are celebrating the day Lu finally got her clothes back!"

I look at her blankly.

Paige guffaws and Lu hides her face in her hands. "Lauren!" she groans.

"What?" I ask.

"Lu's luggage got lost on our flight here," Lauren explains. "But luckily it found its way back to her today. One day more and one of us would have to go naked."

We all laugh and Lu smiles shyly. "I swear I'll wash these tonight and you can have them back tomorrow," she mumbles and picks at the white blouse she's wearing. "My bag should be at the hotel by now."

Lauren pats her hand. "Don't worry, I was kidding. I always bring a few extra pieces."

I'm probably the only one who thinks that's a shame.

Paige squeals: "No shit! I remember your luggage being like ten or fifteen percent overweight on a flight once. And that was a work trip during which we'd dig up dirt for a week, and virtually do nothing else. I still wonder what you had in your bag!"

"Only the essentials. Also it was my second bag, I checked two."

Everyone chuckles and Lauren takes on a mock serious expression. "You will be thanking me the next time you run out of undies!" she says to Paige.

That cracks even me up.

Also, it makes me picture Lauren in a negligee for some reason, causing me to choke on my shake. Romina is there to tip my head a little until my chin almost rests on my chest to ease my breathing and she quickly wipes away some dribbles from my shirt.

Everyone is suddenly very focused on their food.

Ugh. Not for the first time I'm glad Lauren can't read my mind. It's embarrassing how obsessed I'm with her, and it certainly doesn't seem to be healthy for me.

The rest of lunch goes down well, with the women chatting and me mostly concentrating on not messing up further. The shake really is a blessing because it's so easy to drink, and it leaves space for me to join in the conversation from time to time without everyone having to wait for me to finish my food in the end.

"What are your plans tomorrow?" Paige asks. "I checked our flight schedule. We still have time after the conference, right?"

Lauren explains about the exhibition she and I plan to visit.

"Sounds cool." Paige plops the last sushi roll from her plate into her mouth. "Mind if we join you?"

Lauren looks at me and doesn't answer, but that is enough of a clue for me. My heart rate accelerates instantly and I try to open my mouth but have no idea what I'm going to say. My left fist pounds against the side of my wheelchair while my teeth feel glued together.

"It sounds interesting..." Lu says slowly. "Though... all the wasting food... It's probably a little disgusting, right?"

With a strangled gasp I manage to unclench my jaw, which effectively draws all attention to me. "That's... possible. Decaying organics..." I say with more than the usual effort, "I admit... can be... unpleasant."

Lauren watches the table in front of her, smiling to herself as Romina repeats with a frown, concentrating but ultimately failing at stringing my words together to form proper sentences.

"Then it's not for me," Lu decides when she gets the gist and hugs herself, visibly shuddering.

"Oh, that doesn't bother me," Paige announces and wipes her hand on a napkin, pushing her empty plate away with the other. "I took samples from a sewage treatment plant last year. My olfactory nerves are pretty dead, I guess."

"Oh, but..." Lauren says and lifts her head abruptly. "Didn't you want to check out that... *other* museum that I talked to you about." She fixes Paige with her eyes who frowns confused for a second, then looks from Lauren to me and drops her jaw. "Oh..."

"What other museum?" Lu asks, confused, but Paige shakes her head at her and Lu lets it go, though still looking puzzled.

Lauren watches me unblinking, grinning, and I feel warmth creeping up my neck.

Paige jumps. "Holy shit, is this the time?" she cries and tucks at Lu's sleeve. "We gotta go!"

Lu checks her phone with a gasp. "We chair a session after lunch break," she hurriedly explains to me as she rises and gathers her purse. "We should be the ones who are on time." She throws a few bills on the table.

"Yes, definitely," Paige affirms while adding bills of her own. "And I'd like to go through the list of speakers again before we start."

"It was nice meeting you," Lu politely says to Romina and me, smiling kindly. Paige nods, her gaze lingering a little longer on me, with a new quality to it.

I try to smile as well and hit a frequently used pre-formed sentence on the screen of my talker. "Nice to meet you, too," the computer voice says. It's not a lie though. Eating with Lauren and her colleagues has been fun and like travelling back in time a few years. "Good luck with your session," I add in my own voice and Romina relays.

"Any last advice for us?" Lu asks Lauren, but Lauren shrugs and gestures at me. "Patrick may have some. He just had a talk yesterday."

Lu turns around to me. "You had a talk?!" she asks incredulously, then blushes. "I mean... Uh, I didn't..." She blushes even deeper and looks around the group searching for help but Lauren isn't budging.

"Are you a professor?" Paige asks boldly, clearly curious.

"Oh shit...!" Lu claps her hand over her mouth, staring at me wide-eyed.

Lauren laughs. "Don't worry, Patrick is with the industry."

That helps to relax Lu. I do understand her worry of having been overheard by a possible confidant of their supervisors, but I try not to be hurt that they never considered it a possibility. Also, I start to wonder if anyone except Lauren has been to my talk.

"I assume you know your general responsibilities in chairing a session," I say, coming back to the topic at hand. "Just one thing. Try to keep awake during the dullest presentations, since you'll have to pose questions if no one else does."

Paige groans as soon as Romina finishes repeating what I said. "Right, that's the worst!"

Lu's eyes grow big. "And what do I ask if I didn't understand a single thing?"

"You can always ask where they see their research in five years, how it compares to other work in the field that you are more familiar with, or something along the lines," I say.

"Oh good," Lu says and exhales, rolling her shoulders. "I'll try that. Thanks!"

They both wave at me and Romina a little awkwardly, hug Lauren, and quickly leave the restaurant through the front door.

Lauren watches me quietly while I finish the rest of my shake, and once again I am torn between feeling exposed and basking in her attention. She isn't staring like most people do, not with the shame, or fear, or repulsion in her eyes that I usually see if I care to notice people watching me. She just seems mildly interested, and generally content.

"Was it okay?" she asks once I'm done and points to the empty glass that Romina placed on the table.

"Delicious," I exaggerate with a fleeting grin while Romina wipes my chin. It wasn't half bad though. Much better than any other available alternative in this restaurant for sure.

Lauren grins, signaling to Romina that she understood that. Lauren already finished her shake long ago and stole a few sushi rolls from Lu as her colleague was on a bathroom break.

"Your colleagues are nice," I type.

"They are. They weren't too much, were they?" Lauren asks a little worriedly.

"They are lovely," I assure her.

A text message from my brother pops open on my screen and I skim it before swiping it away with a knuckle, sighing. He congratulated me on almost becoming chapter president, followed by a very big smiley face and several thumbs up.

"Bad news?" Lauren asks, one eyebrow raised.

"Just my brother," I answer in my own voice. Lauren seems to become better at understanding me, as long as I only use a small number of words.

Lauren props her chin in her hands. "Younger or older?"

"Younger."

"And annoying."

"Terribly."

Lauren laughs.

I ask Romina to pay the bill and she does, adding my money to the small pile. I tried to invite Lauren but she ignored the hint. "Do you have siblings?" I ask Lauren through Romina.

"I have a younger brother, too," Lauren says. "And an older brother. I got the worst from both."

"My sincerest sympathy."

Lauren chuckles.

We take the same route on our way out as we took in, passing by the bathrooms and the guy behind the desk in the foyer before exiting into the hot, humid air outside.

"I feel like taking a detour to walk along the shore. What do you say?" Lauren asks.

I'd love to, more than anything. Not only would it extend my time with Lauren, but the breeze from the sea must be heavenly right now. However, there isn't much time left until the next session starts and I need to stop by my hotel room before and stretch. A whole day sitting in the wheelchair is killing my body. My entire left side is tight and the pain has risen above its usual dull level, throbbing sharp through my hip and back. I'm going to have to ask Romina for stronger pain medication, but I know that I need to give my body rest for at least a few minutes if I don't want to get knocked out either by pain or by the meds by early evening.

None of this I feel like revealing to Lauren right now.

"I'm sorry, I have appointments," I say between slightly clenched teeth as my lower back tightens up even more when I try turning my head to look at Lauren. It isn't a lie, I have appointments later in the day, just not now.

"Oh, okay," Lauren nods as Romina relays, a little disappointed but not dejected. "See you tomorrow then," she says lightly and lifts a hand in goodbye, turning to go the other way, into the direction of the shore.

"Or maybe... tonight?" I venture, following an impulse. I can't bear to see her walk away and the prospect of passing a lonely evening in my hotel room, with Romina taking a well-earned rest in the adjacent room, seems suddenly very daunting.

Lauren stops and turns around again, her eyes lighting up but the next moment she sighs as something occurs to her. "We have dinner with the group tonight. With my boss and everyone."

"Ah." I'm sure she can't skip that. I attempt to sit a little straighter by pushing my right hand against the armrest, hoping to alleviate the ache in my back. Maybe after dinner...

"My boss usually invites us for cocktails after," Lauren adds before I can open my mouth again.

Guess that settles it. "Well then, tomorrow it is," I say, trying to smile through the pain and the disappointment. Probably it's better to give my body some rest tonight, though.

"Yes. I can't wait," Lauren says quickly, flashing a huge smile, and then walks down the street, her colorful skirt fluttering behind her, her braid swinging in her back.

"Can we go now?" Romina sounds amused but also a little impatient. I feel immediately guilty because I know this lunch meeting has reduced her own break from work to probably a few minutes after stretching.

I duck my head and wrench the joystick to one side, making the powerchair turn its back to Lauren. But the entire way to the hotel I fail to feel outright miserable, despite the pain lashing out at my tortured body every time I get jostled by an uneven stretch in the pavement or a curb, and despite Romina's tired silence at my side. Lauren's joyful smile and her blazing eyes are frozen in my mind like a photo I took the moment before she turned to go. All I can think of are her fingers touching my arm, gently, and as if it was nothing out of the ordinary. But above all that, I have a distinct feeling that my meet-up with Lauren tomorrow may have just become a date of sorts.

CHAPTER 9

By the end of the day I'm properly exhausted and my body is taking revenge on me with increasing spasms, but at least the pain medication is having an effect. After a bland dinner at my hotel I retreat to my room and answer some emails I received from people after my talk. It's fun and relaxes me, and most importantly it takes my thoughts off of Lauren. Not that I don't like thinking about her in general. But having no prospect of seeing her tonight, it just makes me sad.

I know what I would do if Romina weren't in the adjacent room with the baby monitor turned on in case I need anything, and if I had the required equipment within my reach. I realize that the only thing to truly improve my situation would be to have a proper wank, so to speak. But while I can do that at home, with some preparation on the side of my aides, I never thought to reserve space in my already comprehensive luggage to bring a sex toy or two.

My original plan was to retire to bed early but after an hour of writing and sending emails I receive a reply to an email I previously sent. It's from a certain Colin Curtbell, who – judging from the signature of his email – is a professor in the UK. He writes a witty remark to my answer, and I send back a joke, which results in us trading comments and ideas back and forth. It isn't long until we find out that we are staying in the same hotel and Colin suggests that we meet in the hotel bar.

I swear I didn't make this easy for myself. If it weren't for Lauren still lodged in my brain, equal parts happy and sad with longing, and very effectively keeping me from feeling sleepy, I definitely wouldn't have said yes to Colin. My body's condition doesn't allow for many drawn-out days, and while I went to bed late yesterday, today wasn't a walk in the park either. My muscles are even tighter than usual, my left arm is contracted, the curled hand shivering close to my chest, and my right hand is barely cooperative enough to write the emails I'm working on. My knees are locked and pressed together, and I can literally feel my crooked spine struggling against gravity. But only thirty minutes later my lips are pressed together in determination as the powerchair hums its way down the carpeted corridor, toward the elevators.

I know I should rest but there's no relaxation in sight with Lauren perpetually on my mind. I'm tired and miserable and I need some distraction. Romina knows where I'm going and she graciously offered to accompany me, but I don't think it's necessary to stretch my aide's patience even further. Today she has already worked more hours for me than her contract allows and she deserves an evening off. So, all I did was swallow another pain medication, some powder mixed into water, while avoiding her reproachful look. Romina knows just as much as I do that I'm not treating my body in an advisable manner, but to my surprise she held back the lecture. As the wheelchair approaches the elevators, I promise to myself to return before midnight, to get at least one night of proper sleep.

My own stubbornness has me stranded in front of the elevators for a full ten minutes because I don't manage to press the call button. All I accomplish is first ramming a wheel into the wall, then limply knocking the back of my hand against the button with no real effect other than feeling increasingly inept. Maybe I should just have stayed in my hotel room, with my baby monitor and my lift, because even something as simple as going down to the hotel bar to get a drink seems outside my realm of possibility.

Before I can turn the powerchair around and roll back to my room to admit my defeat, the elevator dings and the doors open. A tall woman exits, only taking a quick, startled look at me. Her name tag indicates that she's attending the same conference as I am. I swiftly steer the powerchair into the large and empty cubicle of the elevator before the doors can close again. It's all gold and shiny railings and there's a seemingly old, purposely almost blind mirror on the back wall that I consciously avoid looking at. For a moment I wonder how I'll reach the equally tricky buttons on the wall to my left to tell the elevator that I want to get to the ground level, but before I can despair once more, the cubicle starts moving downward, rumbling slightly.

I'm lucky because it's close to the end of dinner time, so the elevator spits me out on the ground floor, where I steer the wheelchair through a small group of onlookers waiting, shocked into silence by my appearance. I follow a handful of guys to the bar, one person holding the heavy door open for me as they notice me, and this time I'm glad for people's persistent need to help.

Only then do I notice that I have no idea how to recognize Colin. I know he's been to my talk but so have many others, and as far as I remember he didn't pose the question we've discussed via email during the public part of the talk. The bar area in front of me isn't crowded, but people are steadily flowing in, swerving around my wheelchair that is parked right after the entrance while I try to find a face I may recognize.

Fortunately, I'm not exactly hard to spot myself. "Hi!" A voice behind me sounds, slightly nervous, and when I turn the wheelchair around, I realize that I've indeed met Colin in person before. He's the friendly black-haired guy with the funny bow-tie, one of the few people who dared to speak to me after my talk, and who had actually been nothing but courteous.

We grab a nearby table and Colin moves one of the heavy leather chairs to the side to make space for my wheelchair. He sits across from me at the small table, smiling shyly. The bow-tie is gone and he's wearing a plain button-up shirt to blue jeans, which makes him look several years younger. "I'm glad we can continue our discussion in person," he says. "It's um... easier, isn't it?"

While that may be true for him, it certainly isn't for me. For me, it's almost the same, with the added bonus of being on display for everyone in the bar. But I don't say that. "Yes," says the monotone voice of the talker.

"So..." Colin clears his throat and picks up the menu. He may just have realized that he'll mainly be in charge of driving this conversation forward. "What will you have?"

I blink because I actually forgot that people are supposed to drink something in a bar. Right. "I'll have a Virgin Caipirinha," I write, but when the talker reads it aloud, the word 'Caipirinha' is absolutely unrecognizable. I truly wonder who programmed this voice.

Just as well, Colin stares at me in confusion. "A what?" he asks, chuckling nervously.

I turn the screen with some effort, and Colin squints at the words on it.

"Oh!" He laughs. "Of course."

"Yeah," I say without the talker. Then I turn the screen around again and write: "Not the most sophisticated machine."

"Doesn't appreciate cocktails, I'd say," Colin agrees. He pauses, then adds rather thoughtfully: "Do you mind if I drink something stronger?"

Of course I don't. I would drink alcohol if it weren't for the pain killers currently coursing through my veins. There's only so much additional strain I dare to put onto my body.

The waitress arrives and Colin orders a pisco sour. I select my order from the last used words on the talker and turn the screen to let the waitress read.

While we wait for our drinks, Colin and I pick up our conversation where we left it. I can sense Colin had expected our meeting to go differently. Swifter, mostly. Sometimes that happens. People I've already met briefly and who know about my disability and what it implies for me, at least to some extent, seem to suffer some kind of amnesia when I'm not around anymore and when we only have contact through text. Because they don't know how long it takes for me to write an email, and they forget that it takes exactly as long for me to talk to them through the talker, they somehow start to reduce my disability to a minor side note. While that's something I welcome in general, people starting to see more than the wheelchair, it's also painful to witness when that overly optimistic version of me gets corrected in their minds.

After some initial awkwardness, though, with Colin fidgeting and clearing his throat as I type my part of the conversation – and him getting clearly panicked when a small spasm attack pins me to the backrest of my chair, small grunts leaving my gaping mouth – we manage. Once I've convinced my limp right hand to return to the screen and go on with the conversation like nothing happened, Colin takes that as a signal to relax a little. Thankfully I'm having a good day with my face and mouth otherwise, and saliva only where it belongs, because that's certainly where I draw the line for venturing out without my aides.

The waitress brings our drinks and places them on the small table between us. With a reluctant groan I keep her from rushing away again and type the request for her to place the glass into the cup holder and adjust it for me. She does what I asked her for and thankfully doesn't seem too flustered by any of it, not even as my left arm accidentally brushes her thigh as it twitches suddenly.

"Sorry," I type, because I never assume anyone knows just how little control I have over that limb.

She smiles kindly and doesn't seem bothered. "Don't worry. Are you all set now?"

I observe the arrangement and notice that the waitress even thought of turning the straw in my direction. I nod at her, flashing a smile, and try to get a glimpse of her name tag to be able to shower her with praise should I get around to writing a review of the hotel.

There's a lull in the conversation, longer than before, while we are occupied with our drinks. Colin's gaze wanders lazily around the room, but he doesn't give the impression that he's searching for someone more fun than me to pass the evening with.

"Could you stir my drink?" I ask after a while, because while the waitress was very thoughtful about the straw, she didn't think of that. Currently most sugar is at the bottom of the glass and some of it hasn't even dissolved properly yet.

"Oh, uh... yes, sure," Colin stammers, and tentatively leans forward to grab my straw and stir with it. "Like that?"

I grunt in affirmation and thank him. He doesn't answer but instead watches me capture the straw between my lips after a few failed attempts, my head jerking slightly, my left knee jumping under the table, making the wheelchair sway. I pull at the straw and concentrate on swallowing properly, before my upper body rocks backward, audibly punching a pained groan out of my chest.

"How..." There's that sadness in Colin's eyes that I know already and my heart sinks a little. Here it comes. The inevitable. "How do you...? I mean..." He swallows and places his glass on the table, his fingers tapping the table lightly.

How do you do it? How do you get out of bed each morning? How do you live like this? It would require a giant data center to keep track of how often I've been asked that. I square my chest and try not to come off too annoyed. Colin looks at me, then clears his throat and shakes his head. "To be honest, I never understood how you drew the parallels between your work and the Kopenhagen team's research. Could you explain to me—" He falters when he catches me gaping at him, but I reign myself in, kinda wave my hand, and he goes on.

He's a good guy.

We spend some more time discussing work but after half of his cocktail, Colin becomes more forthcoming. I learn he has a Chilean wife with British roots, which is why he moved to the UK for her. He also has two young kids and claims he has been more productive during the last couple of days at the hotel than over the course of the last few years at home. Also, he shares his hotel room with a British colleague who decided to join the conference late and couldn't find a place to sleep.

"We have two beds, luckily" Colin says, chuckling. "I can hear him snore all night, though, you won't believe how loud that is." Said colleague is out with a certain female Biologist tonight, Colin adds with a smirk.

I chuckle, Lauren appearing back in the forefront of my mind. Have they finished dinner already and moved on to drinks? I wonder what Lauren ordered. Does she think about me, too, or am I completely forgotten?

"What's on your agenda tomorrow?"

There are some talks I'd like to attend and the first meeting of the planning committee for next year's conference, which unfortunately I have to attend as vice-president of our chapter. And then there's the date with Lauren, of course, but I don't mention that.

Colin already knows I've been elected and he congratulates me. I make a sour face that has him laugh. "I know what you mean, Patrick." He jiggles the ice cubes in his drink. They clink softly against each other. "At least you don't have to sit in on endless job interviews. I think that's all I'll do tomorrow before catching the first plane in the afternoon."

Many people use the conference to scope out job opportunities. Universities and companies alike usually conduct a number of job interviews, since this is a unique chance to meet so many highly educated people within a short time frame.

"Any promising candidates?" I ask politely. I hate recruiting. Picture me in a regular job interview and you know why. There's nothing worse than having a candidate stare at you the entire time, knowing that the most important question on their mind is if this guy is for real or if someone is having a very cruel joke with them. I avoid situations like that as much as I can.

Colin scrutinizes his empty cocktail glass. "Far too many," he admits. "In theory they are all well suited. It's hard to know who will actually fit in, though. You know what I mean?"

The conversation continues to roll lightly, with me typing and Colin talking more and more animatedly. He tells me that he never had a better pisco sour than the one prepared by his mother in law, and that it can't compare to the Peruvian pisco sour, and for a while he wonders aloud what type of pisco they used in his drink. It's his second cocktail and he isn't drunk enough or ruthless enough to track down our busy waitress to ask her about it.

A while later, Colin excuses himself for a few minutes to call his family from his phone. Once he's gone I hesitate, thinking about sending a message to Lauren. I wonder if I'm coming on too strong, if I'll appear clingy, but then I send a text to Lauren, telling her about the apparently not too bad pisco sour offered at this bar and asking her if she wants to join us. I promise to throw a round for her and everyone in her company, hoping she'll be able to convince her colleagues to come here, too. This would allow her to keep her social obligation to stay with them, I hope.

Upon his return, Colin chugs a third pisco sour and starts humming to the music, his fingers drumming out the beat on the table. The bar apparently offers karaoke in the evening, because a few slightly buzzed people take the small stage in one corner and start singing very confidently and not too terribly into the microphone propped up there.

Colin grins at me. "Do you like music?"

I tell him that I do, and we exchange favorite bands and songs. The music ramps up a little and I start to feel comfortable, the painkillers thankfully numbing the pain enough that it stays at the back of my mind, the music thrumming through my body instead. When I disregard the fact that my left arm's occasional jerk and my head knocking into the backrest are absolutely unintentional, I could pretend I'm just moving to the music, enjoying the rhythm.

"Oh! This is my song!" Colin cries and jumps up. "Bear with me, I have to do this," he apologizes to me and runs off to make his way between the armchairs and tables to the stage. He pulls the microphone toward himself and sings along with a Spanish song that I don't recognize, but it may not be entirely my fault. Even though I have zero musical talent or education it seems highly unlikely to be as consistently out of tune as Colin is, with as much heartfelt conviction and vigor as he sings at the same time. His voice breaks at the height of the song, but he beams and starts the next line with doubled effort, disregarding the exaggerated groans and laughter from the crowd. Thankfully, when the song has ended, he joins me at the table again, flushed and slightly sweaty, but happy.

"Ah..." he sighs as he sits down, his eyes shimmering. "That was the song that played when we first met, my wife and I, in a little bar in Santiago." He brings out his phone and flips it between his hands, then sighs. "Is it crazy that I miss her and the children, after just a few days? Talking to them on the phone just isn't the same."

When Colin mentioned his wife, I felt the pang of loss at not being with Lauren right now, and I know exactly what he means. After all, Lauren and I saw each other just a few hours ago.

For the umpteenth time I check my messages but no reply from her.

"I tell you what," Colin says, leaning over the table to me. "I never thought I would end up with my wife, you know. She is..." He closes his eyes for a moment and lifts his hands a little. "She's perfect, absolutely perfect. Gorgeous. Intelligent. Courageous. And still..." He shrugs. "She wanted me. Wants me. Even though I'm... just a regular guy." He gestures at himself and I must admit for a moment I struggle with getting his meaning. He's pretty average, yes. Not handsome, not ugly. Not exceptionally boring, but also not very exciting. He's a guy you'd probably forget about quite quickly after meeting him. He's basically everything I'd kill for.

Colin sighs. "Well, I'm not complaining. But we almost missed each other in that bar and if she hadn't talked to me first, I would never have made the move, and we would never have gotten married. But enough of that," he suddenly says, grinning at me crookedly. Maybe he noticed I'm definitely not the right audience for this. "Why are we so serious? This is a great place, a great night!" He gestures at me and our surroundings. "We should enjoy it, don't you think?"

I nod slowly but before I can type something, a couple of guys come over to our table. They either know Colin or have witnessed his performance at karaoke and want to congratulate him ironically. Or both. They clap his back and squeeze my shoulder, and make a few bawdy jokes. One starts a discussion about something vaguely related to research, shouted in a very drunk accent at no one in particular, but gets called off by Colin. "Stop that nonsense and let's go singing," Colin says, and staggers off with them to the stage.

For a moment I stare at my empty cocktail glass, the noise of the bar roaring in my ears, then I jumpstart the wheelchair. A waiter opens the doors for me to slip through and the sound from the bar gets dimmed as they close softly behind me. My knuckle shivers over the screen, nerves getting the better of me and I wonder if it's the lack of sleep and heightened level of pain medication that has me do a very unwise thing. Before I can chicken out, I close my eyes and hit Lauren's number.

It rings three times before Lauren answers. She seems slightly out of breath and giddy, as if she just stopped laughing to answer the phone. "Hi, Patrick!"

I try to ignore the nervous jolt in my stomach and inhale. "I can't stop thinking about you," I say despite my better judgement, forcing myself to talk as slowly and clearly as I can manage.

The background noise on Lauren's side fades, as if she stepped away from the crowd or shields her phone with her hand. "Can you repeat that?" she says, her voice completely sober.

I swallow, my heartbeat hammering in my ears. At first, I'm not sure I can bring up the strength required to repeat myself, but then I manage to find some courage. "I c-can't..." I say, pretending I don't notice how badly I'm doing. I wait until Lauren confirms with a hum. "... stop thinking..." My left foot pushes into the footrest, making my upper body slide to the right in the molded seat until it's caught by the strap around my chest, a strangled sound escaping me. "ngh... about you...".

"You can't stop..." Lauren repeats slowly, still figuring things out, "You can't stop thinking... about me...?" She says the last part like a question and I don't know if she isn't sure she understood me correctly or if she doesn't know what to make of it.

"I'm sorry," I add, trying to enunciate clearly. This time it works better. "I was just calling to..." My mouth snaps shut with a facial spasm. Defeated, I resort to typing, unsure if the voice of the talker will be picked up by the speaker of my phone. I never call anyone except maybe my aides, and that only in an emergency. "I had to hear your voice."

"I'm glad I could hear yours, too," Lauren says quietly after a short silence. "I like your voice," she adds.

While this can surely just be meant as a polite nicety, it still makes my stomach flutter.

"And geez if only I knew what happened tonight." Lauren sighs and then chuckles. "I probably agreed to a ton of work without knowing because all I could think of was meeting you tomorrow," she says.

"Really?"

"Hmmm..."

"I understand you can't come here tonight," I type and send to the talker. "But I thought I could tell you goodnight. It's probably too early for that, considering it's not that late and also silly, forgive me." I struggle to put everything I want to say into words that don't sound completely stupid coming from the lifeless voice of the talker.

"It's not silly!" Lauren protests, sounding delighted. "It's very sweet of you Patrick. Alas, I'm afraid I can't bid you goodnight just now."

"Why not?"

There's no answer from her side and I tap the screen to make sure I haven't broken the connection by accident, when I hear the quick sound of heels behind me just a split second before something covers my eyes.

"That's why," Lauren's voice says into my ear, not from the speakers but from right next to my head. She lifts her hands off my eyes and laughs as she steps around the powerchair and in front of me.

I can only stare at her. She's wearing a short, dark blue dress and her hair is down and curling over her shoulders. Her perfume is engulfing me and that alone would make me smile with how familiar it is to me by now. Alas, I'm pretty much incapable of doing anything, let alone move a single finger for a few painful moments, because she startled me and my body doesn't react well to that. My muscles have seized up, locking me in a position looking at a first delighted, then puzzled Lauren, and they only begin to loosen by the time Lauren's colleagues have caught up with her. I recognize Lu and Paige, and there are two young guys that I haven't met before, who all watch me with expressions varying from mild worry to shock.

Finally, my chest expands enough to let me draw a rattling breath and I manage to knock my right hand against the talker. "Hi," the mechanic voice says. I was lucky to hit the intended field at all.

Everyone offers an awkward greeting and I get introduced to the people I haven't met before, but I don't really manage to catch their names because I'm occupied with getting a grip on my revolting body. I'm still out of breath when the group decides to enter the bar and by the time I manage to make the powerchair move, there's only Lauren left at my side.

"Sorry," she whispers a little sheepishly.

I wiggle my head in an attempt to wave it aside. She couldn't have known I'm this easily startled, and what effect it has on me. It is a nice surprise that she came here, though, very nice indeed, and I tell her as much as soon as the group has managed to grab a table near where Colin and I sit. Lauren perches on the arm of Colin's empty chair and watches me type very slowly.

As the talker speaks, Lauren smiles. "Our boss had to go attend an online meeting with Australian colleagues, so I thought we'd come here. Good, huh?"

"I'm glad," I type. "And I meant what I texted you. Drinks on me." I grin as we look at each other probably a second too long. Then I get distracted by a waiter arriving and I manage to fix his gaze before he can take anyone else's orders.

"Yes?" The waiter has his pen poised, watching me with raised eyebrows.

Knowing it will take forever to type my request, I jerk my head at Lauren, staring hard at her until she explains to the waiter that I'll throw a round for her and her colleagues. The waiter nods and collects orders. I receive cheers and thumbs up from Lauren's colleagues at the nearby table.

Colin, who is still with the group of scientists and occupied with karaoke, takes a very unconventional approach to Adele. Lauren giggles. "Holy shit, you didn't mention *this*."

"Oh yes," I say and then type: "That's Colin."

Lauren's eyebrows shoot up and I feel compelled to tell her how I met Colin. Since he and his friends seem determined to sing through the current charts, Lauren sinks into his chair across from me. We talk about the conference, grants and scholarships and our experiences working at university. I tell her about the chapter's meeting this morning and Lauren thinks it's awesome I became vice president. She really seems to believe I could be anything more than lousy in that position and I try to stifle her enthusiasm, without much success.

Lauren doesn't seem to mind the long breaks when I type, doesn't get bored or distracted because the conversation is slow. She leans forward over the table as the singing gets more raucous, to listen closely to the talker's voice. When she's thinking she chews on her lip, and she twists her hair around her finger again. Although she could easily take over most of the conversation, she doesn't. She allows for pauses in her speech long enough for me to indicate I'd like to speak, and waits patiently until I have composed what I want to say.

We are making jokes about the parallels between the chapter's finances and our home city's planning decisions when Colin returns to the table. "I'm sorry to intervene but you're missing all the fun," he says. "Hi, by the way." He turns to Lauren and shakes her hand. "You'll both have to come with me now," he drawls then. He kinda hugs me, trying to pull me upright with him, and it seems to take a few seconds for Colin to register that there's no sense in trying to pull me out of the wheelchair.

"You better uh… drive," he mumbles, waving his hand about, and grabs the armrest as he stumbles a little, catching himself. "Whoops!" He giggles and straightens himself holding on to my shoulder. "Come on, I asked for our song."

I don't have to type because my face speaks volumes, I guess. Lauren suppresses a laugh that comes out as a snort through her nose.

"Our *song*!" Colin repeats, waving his arms. "Everyone needs a song. Trust me, I picked a good one for us. Come on now!"

I try explaining that I can't sing and anyway probably won't be able to access the stage, but Colin isn't listening and before he can try and manipulate the joystick, which I can see he is about to do soon and is only held back by a little shred of common sense and rapidly decreasing patience, I follow him through the packed bar and to the stage. It's a miracle for me unto this day how I manage to get there without running anything or anyone over, but maybe I did and just didn't notice. Lauren follows in our wake. I somehow make it to the stage and when the footrest bumps into the first step Colin seems to notice the flaw in his plan.

He isn't deterred though. He jumps onto the stage, removes the microphone from its stand and hurries down to us. Then he leans down to me a little and yells into the microphone: "This is for everyone here!" just as the guitars and drums start.

"Rising up, back on the street…"

Our song is Eye of the Tiger. I stare at Colin, my mouth a little more open than usual. Is he making fun of me? I continue watching Colin, singing, yelling, screaming, and dancing in a tight circle around us, with the microphone placed under Lauren's and my nose frequently, although I'm not singing. Lauren is, though, and she is miles better than Colin, her voice a little breathy but sweet. As I see the sparkle in her eyes, and Colin's broad grin as he looks at us, I know that this isn't a joke. I start smiling and for all it's worth, as the microphone knocks against my chest the next time, I hum along a little. It's all I can accomplish. When you have difficulties breathing and speaking, it usually isn't an easy fate to sing. No one really seems to notice anyway. After a while, a few of the other guys join us. They throw their arms over each other's shoulders and take Lauren and me into their midst, and Colin's cat noises are drowned out when everyone joins in for the chorus.

We leave the bar much later than I intended, Lauren riding on the armrest with her arm around the back of the wheelchair. She is a grown woman and the armrest is not built for transporting people, but I'm too far gone at this point for rational considerations. As the sound of voices, music, and singing is getting dimmer behind us, I notice all of a sudden just how tired and how much in pain I am. The pain medication has waned and the ache in my back and hip is sharp again. As we advance the elevator, the room is blurring a little, and I notice my ears are ringing in this unusual silence.

We have managed to convince a rather drunk Colin to accompany us, and he calls the elevator while Lauren doesn't seem to want to abandon her position on the armrest. She's so close to me, my contracted left arm brushes against her thigh occasionally, the fabric of her dress smooth and warm against my skin. She's in no danger of being hit by me, the muscles in that limb are so tight by now that my arm has ceased jerking almost entirely and instead resorted to painful trembling.

Colin manages to actually push the button after a few drunken trials, which reminds me of my failed attempts at it before. Seems my usual coordination equals his with decidedly too many cocktails in his system.

No one talks as we wait. Lauren's fingers slip from the headrest and start playing with my hair, absentmindedly. I know my hair may be a little too long, but right now I'm absolutely glad of its length. My entire scalp tingles comfortably and if I were a cat I'd probably purr. I manage to turn my head a little and look at Lauren. Her eyes are half closed and she bites on her lips a little. My dick twitches in my pants. A small groan escapes me as I try to stifle my arousal and, at the same time, pray she may lean closer to me and—

The cubicle arrives with a 'ding' and makes both of us jump, Lauren's eyes flying open. Colin turns around to us. "Time to say goodbye," he drawls, lifting his hand at Lauren, who looks at me and sighs.

I would give all my possessions and my PhD title if I could invite Lauren up into my hotel room now.

Alas, I can't. Romina is in the room next to mine, probably asleep already and pissed at me because I'm much later than I promised. She will have to get up to undress me, wash me and put me to bed, and none of those things I want Lauren to witness.

"Good night," I whisper, only choking a little on the second word. Lauren gives another small, longing sigh, then retreats her hand. As the presence of it vanishes, the stabbing pain in my joints and back increases all of a sudden, like a sharpening picture. I gasp involuntarily and clench my teeth. So much for prolonging this night. Even if I had a hotel room of my own and could reach my bed independently, I desperately need to give my body some rest.

"Good night," Lauren breathes and places a kiss on my cheek that's feathery light and deepens the ache in my heart. Suddenly I have no idea how I'm going to survive an entire night without her. "See you tomorrow," she says, smiling a little as she hops off the armrest.

"Yes," I say, trying to maintain eye contact while steering the wheelchair into the elevator. She stands and looks at the sorry image of me, sunken sideways in the wheelchair and breathing flatly through the pain, until the doors close after a while and the cubicle starts ascending.

Colin giggles about nothing in particular, making me aware of his presence. He has already hit his floor and I ask him to hit mine.

"Hmmm…" Colin makes, his face getting very close to mine, then retreating again. He shakes his head, his eyes narrowed. "Still can't understand you," he says. "Damn."

Right. I dared to speak aloud and even without the exhaustion making everything even harder than it normally is, Colin probably would have his difficulties understanding me. Unfortunately, somehow the talker seems very far out of my reach at the moment. The screen is swimming in front of my eyes and as I stare at my hand lying on the armrest, it feels much too heavy to type anything with.

Thankfully, Colin seems to have sobered up a little. "Which one's your floor?" he asks, and points to the buttons until I give a grunt as a signal. Colin gives me a thumbs up. "See? We can do without your stupid machine."

His joking makes my heart grow a little lighter.

As we stop at my floor, I gesture for him to follow me because it occurred to me I can't enter my hotel room on my own and I'm not sure I'll be able to access the talker and call Romina. Colin catches on fast and indeed follows me out of the elevator.

"You and... Lauren, right?" he says with a lewd grin, ambling alongside me.

I grunt. Lauren and I didn't hide anything, and, apparently, we were rather obvious.

"Well, good luck with her. She seems like a good one."

I nod, smiling a little despite my back screaming at me. At least there's tomorrow. I will see her then. And we'll figure something out for the time after that.

We stop at the door to my hotel room. After a few communication failures, Colin finds my key card in one of the pockets attached to the wheelchair and uses it to open the door, though that takes a few attempts for him, too, and loads of swearing. The process probably wakes up about half of the people sleeping on this floor, but finally the door swings open.

Romina is standing in the frame, in her nightdress and with her arms folded over her chest. "Patrick." Her stern gaze first hits me, then Colin, who cringes.

"Um..." Colin backs away, scratching his neck. He looks from Romina to me, then clears his throat. "Good night, Patrick," he mumbles, suddenly timid. He nods at Romina who hasn't moved an inch, then he vanishes down the corridor toward the elevators, in an almost straight line.

Romina continues glaring at me, without moving a muscle.

I feel every bit like twenty years ago, when I was out after curfew and my mother caught me trying to sneak back home. Instead of Colin slinking away it would be Will, muttering excuses under my mother's angry gaze.

"Sorry," I mumble, trying not to break eye contact with Romina. More than anything, I feel sorry for not being able to bring myself to bed. Still, as I hear Colin drunkenly clatter down the corridor, quietly singing to himself, I can barely hold back a grin and I don't feel so sorry after all. It was a fun night and above all, it was with Lauren. I will pay for it, though, I know that.

Romina sighs and finally steps to the side to let me through. "Alright. But no complaints tomorrow."

I know she means I'll be sore as hell tomorrow and she's probably right. I solemnly swear to her that I won't utter a single word.

CHAPTER 10

I get out of bed in time for the very first talk the next morning, but it's not without a part of me wishing last night hadn't happened. Every movement feels like moving mountains, and even though Romina pumped me up with pain killers, I can still feel the persistent ache pulsing in my back. Thankfully, by the end of the first session, the medication shows some proper effect, and I stop wincing every time my legs kick out. When we switch lecture halls after the coffee break, I begin to feel like this isn't the worst day of my life. Only the second worst. But thinking back to Lauren's fingers on my scalp, it was all worth it, and as promised to my aide, I don't complain.

The conference building is huge and despite of some people still lingering around after the coffee break, all in deep conversation, most conference attendees are already inside the lecture and seminar rooms, so I don't expect to meet Lauren by accident. But just as I cruise down the corridor, I spot her sitting in a corner by the stairs. My heart rate instantly speeds up. She's wearing a black business dress, much more formal than the days before, the red ribbon in her hair the only individual note catching my eyes this time. Her gaze is turned down to her phone and when I approach her I can sense that something is not right.

Lifting my hand off the joystick briefly, I respectfully ask Romina to wait for me in the back, and then steer the wheelchair toward the stairs alone.

Lauren's head flies up as soon as she hears the humming of my chair getting closer and she smiles a bit, but I can see the remnants of tears glistening in the corners of her eyes.

"Hey," I greet her, somewhat lamely because I'm

concentrating on parking with some distance to her, afraid I might bump into her crossed legs if I tried to get any closer.

"Hi..." she says, wiping at her cheeks quickly and squeezing the phone in her hand. "Yesterday was great, wasn't it?"

I nod, but deciding not to play dumb, I ask straight away. "What's wrong?"

For a moment I'm afraid Lauren may not have understood me although I did my best to articulate properly. But then she shrugs and says: "I told you I think about going back home, didn't I?"

I nod. Her current position will end in less than six months and she's looking for further employment options, preferably around the area where she comes from. Around where I live.

Lauren sighs. "Well, I just had a job interview. The company's headquarter would be an hour by car away from my parent's house."

Which means it's probably as close to mine as well. I watch her attentively. It would be awesome if she moved back.

"I totally butchered it."

That comes as a surprise. As intelligent and well-spoken as she was with me, I'd have thought that she would kill every job interview. Not to mention her looks, which should have most men and women lying at her feet, in my opinion. My head wiggles as I continue to look at her, trying to convey with my eyes that I feel sympathy for her and inquiring for more details, while I'm damning my inability to do more. It would have taken way too long to type all of what I want to say on the screen or try to form into words Lauren could understand.

Lauren gets it. She turns her phone around in her hands a few times, then continues. "It's my fault," she says. "I... I've always just panicked in exam situations." She shrugs it off but her posture remains tense. "It was the same back when I was a student and that's why my grades are what they are. I'm lucky anyone even invites me to a job interview. I just..." She blinks away more angry tears and tucks the phone into her black leather business bag. "Everything just goes blank, you know?"

I nod my head, slowly. It's hard for me to picture her like that, but I can see she's truly devastated about it.

Lauren squeezes her hands together, staring at them. "I went into that room and sat in front of that desk, and there was this guy and a woman, looking at me like they were about to grade me and I... I just lost it."

More tears start running down Lauren's cheeks and I feel so damn helpless in that moment, strapped into the wheelchair and unable to do even something as simple as reaching out with my hand to squeeze her quivering shoulders.

"I'm... sorry," I manage to say, slurring like crazy. From a lack of reaction on her side, I honestly doubt Lauren understood me, though. My right fist shivers into action and leans over to the talker to type on the screen. Although I try to be quick it takes forever, the muscles in my arm are tightening up the more effort I put into it.

"Shit, I'm... I'm sorry that I'm telling you all that," Lauren says when nothing comes from me, sniffing her tears back up and averting her face. It's like a slap across my cheek. She grabs her bag and gets up to leave. "I guess you don't need to hear it." She isn't looking at me as she all but flees the scene.

"Wait," I try calling after her despite my own reservations against using my voice in public, but my throat is seizing and nothing articulate comes out. Still, Lauren stops mid-step and turns to me, almost dutifully and against her own will. I swallow my irritation at that, at almost everything, and steer the wheelchair closer to her, away from the secluded spot at the side of the stairs. A guy appears out of nowhere and almost crashes into us while he has his nose in his phone. He apologizes profusely and repeatedly to me and disappears. I don't waste a second thought on it, desperately trying to find something that will make Lauren listen to me and doesn't take too long to type out. "Do you see a therapist?" the talker says.

I didn't manage to phrase it less blunt, but it certainly serves the intended purpose. Lauren looks at me like I just asked her if she can do a handstand on my shoulders. "What?!"

I know that look and I scroll through the quick-selection section, searching for something. "Coffee." I turn the chair around on the spot, heading down the corridor and essentially away from the coffee corner situated inside the conference building. I'm heading for a more private spot.

I can only hope Lauren is following me, and indeed her elbow appears in my line of sight. "Where are we going?" she asks.

I jerk my head to the exit and wait for her to hold the door open so that I can roll through. Before I do, I angle the chair back a bit. "See you in a bit, please?" I ask Romina who has followed us in surprisingly respectful distance. She stops and frowns, letting her eyes glide from us to the outside. She could take revenge on me for waking her up in the middle of the night by making this complicated, but instead she nods and lets herself fall behind.

The wheelchair bumps over a miniscule ledge and onto the thankfully wide and even sidewalk. I go a bit easier on the joystick, aware of the cars rushing past us narrowly. The air outside is moist and warm and my shirt starts to stick to my skin almost immediately.

Lauren has been surprisingly patient but now she begins to get restless. "Patrick, what the heck—"

But we've already rounded the corner and stop in front of an outside coffee stand. It's not the best coffee but there's never a queue, due to the climate outside and also because conference people usually don't like to walk very far. For me it's the perfect place to get a bit of peace. It's not my first time at this venue and I had figured these things out rather quickly.

"Oh..." I hope that's Lauren understanding I was trying to find a secluded spot for us to talk properly, before the building gets flooded with people upon the next break.

As I steer the wheelchair to the high counter, Lauren follows me. "Um... how do you take your coffee?" she asks when the guy behind the counter looks down at us expectantly.

"Black, without sugar," the guy says and grins at me. "Hi Patrick!"

One of the perks of being me is that everyone will remember

every detail about you once they've met you. For years.

It's also one of my pet peeves.

Luckily I have a good memory for peoples' names and faces. "Mike..." I drawl and jerk my head into a greeting.

Mike beams happily. "And the lady?"

"Um... with milk and sugar, please," Lauren says. She ends up paying because Romina has my money but I try not to feel too bummed out by it. I hope I can pay her back soon.

Lauren carries the two paper cups over to one of the empty sets of tables and chairs. I park between two wide-spaced chairs and she gets into a plastic chair across from me.

"Um..."

My coffee has a straw in it but I would need her to either put it in the cup holder and adjust the flexible arm that is attached to it to the right height or hold it up for me to reach it. "It's too hot," I type on the screen instead. "Enjoy yours."

Lauren blows into her coffee and sips from the dark brown liquid in her cup, relaxing a bit into the seat for the first time. I use the break to type more. "Tell me from the beginning. If you want."

Lauren sighs. "What's there to tell? I... You know what?" She crosses her arms in front of her chest. "I'm so pathetic, I have no idea how I even got a PhD! Certainly not because I shone in the examination. Someone in my committee must have had a heart or something... I only got my current position because the internet connection wasn't good enough for a proper job interview via video, I presume, and my current boss and I chatted using the text messenger. That... that was easier, somehow. And then today... ugh..." She looks like she's going to start crying again.

I really wish I could somehow comfort her physically. I'd put my arm around her shoulders and let her lean against my chest but there's no way for me to do this on my own. "Is it the exam-like situation?"

Lauren nods, her lips a straight line.

There's enough time for me to compose the next sentence.

"This sounds serious, Lauren. I wasn't joking before."

Lauren winces and laughs stiffly. "Uh huh… it's not that bad."

I stare at her and she rolls her eyes but blushes. "Okay, yes… it is, maybe. But it shouldn't be such a problem, alright? If I could just wrap my head around it and stay calm like any normal person… It's not that I usually fear talking to people or talking about my work. I love my work! It's just… I don't know, I can't do it in a situation like that." She groans. "It shouldn't be so hard, damn!"

I nod, slowly. "Doesn't matter. It's hard for you."

"It shouldn't be," she repeats stubbornly.

My head is thrown around too much to hold eye contact for long, so I give up on fixing my gaze on Lauren. "You want that job, right?" I manage to type when my body gives me a few shreds of control back.

Lauren sighs and stares at the table. "Yeah…" she admits.

"Then do something about it. You know that you could get help?"

Lauren rubs her forehead. "I know… I just don't want to." She sighs again. "I could've gotten extended time for writing exams back when I was a student at university and I always refused because I don't want to be singled out, you know? I don't want to be the poor kid that gets special treatment because something is wrong with her. I don't want to get a job offer out of pity and I don't want to have to see a stupid therapist!" She grabs her cup and angrily sips her coffee.

"I have a business meeting to attend in ten minutes," I type.

Lauren looks disappointed for a moment but then she nods, about to get up again.

"I prepared a presentation for the meeting," I continue because I'm not finished yet, it just took a long time to write. Lauren stills, frowning at me, confused, but waiting now patiently.

"I want to give it myself, standing up, writing things on the whiteboard like the other people at the meeting. I want to answer questions directly. I want to eat a sandwich or a salad, if the meeting lasts through lunch." My head gets thrown back by spasms, bumps against the headrest and knocks a pained groan out of my chest. I authorize the rest of the text being sent to the speakers with some delay. "But I can't do any of it. The talker will give the speech. I'll have another nutrition shake, probably. And like always, Romina will relay what I say."

Lauren blinks at me and plops back in her chair. "Gosh, I'm sorry..." she whispers, her cheeks growing rosy with embarrassment. "Geez, and here I was—"

I lift my hand quickly to stop her from saying what I very well know she wants to say, inwardly cringing already. It's difficult to return my hand to the screen again after that but I manage with utmost concentration. "I'm not saying I've got it harder than you," I hurry to write. "It's not about that. But look, I don't want to do this either. This conference thing. You think I enjoy being stared at the entire time?"

In fact, usually my brother is the one who goes to events like these because I'm glad to take any opportunity not to have to go. I guess I've argued with him about it enough already. So yep, who am I to talk to Lauren about that? The thing is, I get where she's coming from, I truly do, but I also know that sometimes you have to take the bitter pill. I have my brother to kick me in the ass for that and I figure Lauren needs someone like that, too.

Yes, I know the kicking part might be hard for me to accomplish, thank you very much.

I shrug, sort of, before sending the last part to the talker. "Events like this are a vital part of my work and have led to so many beneficial encounters, it wouldn't really be possible without it. So, it's either doing it in a way that I don't like or not doing it at all. You've got to make that decision."

Lauren ponders over that. "Shit..." she says after a while and throws her empty coffee cup in the bin. She places her elbows on the table, chin in her hands. She looks still pissed, but now she's grinning a tiny bit. "I guess you're right. Damn."

Reflexively, I smile as well. "I know... how you feel," I add in my own voice, abandoning the talker and ploughing through the vowels like I am trying to win a prize. I really want her to get this. "It's not... easy."

Lauren sighs and squeezes my right underarm, which, to my surprise, holds relatively still for the short moment it lasts. "Ugh... yeah, I assume it isn't. Thanks. Thanks for sharing."

"Now get me the coffee," the talker reads and I try winking at her. At the same time I try not to think about how it felt again when she touched me, her soft fingers closing around my arm, warm and tingling... I want her to touch my arm again, I want her to touch me in all kinds of other places, too.

Lauren chuckles and grabs my cup, holding the straw up to my lips. I'm glad she doesn't seem to be sad anymore. Maybe my little speech has indeed helped.

"I thought you have to be at a meeting about now, Mr. Vice President?"

I roll my eyes, my legs quivering. She's right though. "They'll wait." I think of the many more meetings I'll have to attend in the future, of Theodore Hebert's icy glare, and stifle a sigh. "They need to get used to waiting anyway."

CHAPTER 11

Shortly after noon, Lauren picks me up in front of my hotel, just as we'd agreed. Luckily my meeting hadn't lasted as long as I had feared, mainly because Hebert had ignored me throughout the entire time. Lauren has changed from her colorless business outfit and is wearing a red dress with white dots, carrying a leather bag slung over her shoulder and pulling her already packed suitcase behind herself. Her dark brown hair is tied into a high ponytail, the tips swinging against her neck. She gives me an adorable smile as a greeting and kisses my cheeks, her perfume enveloping me as she bends down.

Romina and Lauren have had a long discussion on the phone before. I know because I had been in the adjacent room in the hotel, to which we retreated after my meeting had ended. I was working on my nutrition shake that Romina had placed into the cup holder on my wheelchair and positioned high enough so that I could reach the straw myself. At the same time I answered texts from Colin, who had written to me several times to apologize about getting wasted yesterday and to inquire about my wellbeing. I told him he had nothing to apologize for and thanked him for escorting me back to my hotel room. I assured him that last night had been very enjoyable, and that Romina had ripped my head only half off, which wouldn't make much of a difference anyway. Still, I couldn't help but listen to every single bit of Romina's and Lauren's conversation. They spoke about certain details of my condition, what I'd need assistance with (almost everything) and what I'd manage on my own (not much), and a couple of warning signs at which Lauren was to immediately call one of the emergency numbers that Romina dictated to her.

As I overheard the crash-course I was almost ready to call it all off. Who would go out with someone who could choke on their own vomit while being fully conscious? Just hearing Romina talk about all the catastrophic eventualities made me sick. No one in their right mind would want to have to bother with that.

Before we get into the wheelchair-accessible taxi, Romina explains to Lauren how the attendant controls of my wheelchair work and I try my best not to get disgruntled as the two women manipulate my chair, making it jolt forward and halt abruptly, the strap around my chest digging into flesh and the fingers of my right hand twitching to stop them messing around. Thankfully, Lauren proves herself a fast learner. She also passes the quiz that Romina fires at her without a single error while the taxi driver stands next to us with the doors of his car already open, unashamedly observing the spectacle.

If she doesn't think that any of this is weird, I don't know what's wrong with her. But I'm not complaining. The taxi driver stands around uselessly while Romina steers my wheelchair over the ramp into the van and fastens the chair using the various straps in the car. Lauren turns around in the front passenger seat, smiling at me with a happy sparkle in her eyes as soon as I am all set up. I still can't get over the thought that maybe she indeed enjoys looking at me as much as I do looking at her.

That has been the only reason why I've not bailed this afternoon. I wanted to see Lauren again before I leave, even if it's a pain in the ass for all of us to make it possible and although I know I'll pay dearly for not giving myself a bit of rest after the last stressful days. On top of everything I still feel self-conscious and scared on the prospect of going on a date so quickly, but I want to be able to look into her face and see her smile, just for a few more hours.

Plus, I also like art. I would probably not have used my last afternoon at the conference to visit a museum but I'm not completely opposed to it.

We enter the large museum building through broad

automatic doors. "That'll be 11.50 for you, sir," the lady behind the counter says in a voice that is flat with indifference. She doesn't look at me, though, instead she talks to Lauren who is standing right next to me.

Lauren hesitates, her purse in her hands.

"Aides get a free pass," the lady explains in a bored tone and with a fleeting look at me, slightly suspicious at the fact that Lauren doesn't seem to know that.

"Oh, uh... right... I know." Lauren blinks and hurriedly hands over the money that Romina gave her for my entrance ticket. She cocks an eyebrow at me while she receives the change. "Too weird," she whispers into my ear, leaning down a bit as I roll through the wheelchair entrance and deeper into the large, well air-conditioned building.

I smile up at her and inwardly shake my head. Well, if she thinks *that* is weird...

As it turns out, the exhibition is in fact really interesting even from a scientific point of view. Basically every single piece of art in the exhibition is made out of food: food in various stages of decay and rot, some partly conserved and others left to waste away on purpose, the exhibition changing with every day as a result of it. In parts it has a certain morbid quality to it that I find rather fascinating.

Lauren and I spend a long time in front of a large glass frame filled with chocolate that was first melted and then congealed. It takes me a while to steer the wheelchair close to the frame without ramming the wall behind it. We stare at the various types of chocolate forming long strings and globs, black and white and brown melting together, swirling and glistening and ending up in the strangest shapes on their way to the bottom, where a thick layer of chocolate has pooled. It's strangely dark and terrifying, and the longer I look the more detail I discover inside the frame, tiny sculptures and entire landscapes made of chocolate, formed by gravity and pure chance, frozen in time.

It's also pretty disgusting.

"Like looking into a chocolate-loving monster's dietary tract,"

Lauren comments in a whisper, shuddering a bit next to me.

I chuckle. "A three-year-old's stomach after Halloween," I counter.

Lauren looks down at me from the side for a few seconds before she decides she understood me correctly, then laughs. "Exactly, that's what I said."

We're still figuring out the best way of communication between us two, without Romina to relay for me. Typing is good while being stationary, like yesterday night in the bar. It may be appropriate for more complex topics, too, but the talker just isn't made for being used while strolling around. So talking it is, and I work really hard on enunciating as clearly as possible, hoping Lauren will get the gist. So far, it has worked out alright. When Lauren doesn't understand my meaning at all, she tells me the parts that are clear, and I can repeat the words that she missed. I feared it would be endlessly awkward but that's not the case with Lauren. When the guessing game gets too wild, she laughs at herself, stops walking and waits for me to use the talker.

Walking around the exhibition with Lauren is fun and relaxing. We seem to have a shared interest and take similar amounts of time to enjoy a certain piece of art. When we move, Lauren keeps close to me and sometimes briefly places a hand on my shoulder or the underarm that commands the joystick. It's casual and at the same time I feel like she's claiming me, in a good way, because she doesn't seem to mind that there are people around when she does this. And every time she touches me, I feel a soft tingle in my skin, like electric current and I start to wonder if it feels the same for her.

The main piece of art in the exhibition is located in its own hall. It's a giant rotating kitchen, which is one large box that is open just on one side and is suspended in a way that it can rotate around itself the entire time. The furniture inside is fixed to the walls of the box but everything else that must have been on the kitchen table, inside the stove or in the cupboards and shelves, has fallen out and is rumbling around in the box, being tossed from wall to ceiling to wall to floor as the kitchen does yet another and another circulation. The noise is indescribable. A microwave, battered pans and pots and broken china in various forms, shapes and colors, cutlery, soup ladles, food leftovers, carving boards and plastic food containers are sliding along the surfaces and tumbling down the walls, creating a never-ending cacophony of kitchen utensils. The majority of what was inside the kitchen has been transported outside by now, shards and broken parts littering the floor around it, reaching well beyond the line marking the safe distance for visitors.

I'm careful not to get too close to the rotating kitchen and the broken china strewn around it, lest I damage one of the wheels on my chair. Every time the kitchen drawers roll shut or the larger cabinet doors bang close, I jump, startled. The air reeks of spoiled food which is mostly stuck to the insides of the kitchen or spread over the floor close to the rotating box, forming splatters in different shades of red, orange and brown.

Lauren looks at me, wrinkles her nose, and together we quickly leave that hall again.

The next room is full of sculptures made of butter. It's cooled down a lot more than any of the other rooms to preserve the displays. The low temperature is a bit troubling for me, as is the narrow space between the display cases. Lauren slows down with me and trails behind me as I maneuver the wheelchair into the aisle between the sculptures. We don't get far before I narrowly miss the heels of a visitor blocking part of the way. He's almost smudging his nose against the glass of the display case in front of him, which shows a naked woman bathing in the light of an invisible sun. I avoid rolling over his feet with the wheels but my armrest slightly brushes against his side.

The guy turns around, agitated. "Hey, watch where you're go—" His eyes grow wide as his gaze falls down on me. "Oh... Sorry, sir..." His face turns a funny shade of red. "I'm really sorry, I wasn't—"

"My fault," I say.

The guy closes his mouth and stares at me in horror. "Uh..." It's obvious he didn't understand me.

Lauren isn't my aide. I wanted this to be clear before we left. She's only going to assist me with things I absolutely can't deal with on my own. Like doors. Or narrow spaces. But that's basically where her duties at helping end. This is supposed to be a date of sorts. At least I hope it is.

But although Lauren is not my aide, she's actually rather good at substituting Romina. "He said it's his fault," she explains to the guy and steps closer to me, casually slipping one hand on my shoulder.

"Oh um..." The guy looks from Lauren to me and back again, confusion on his face. He pulls his baseball cap off and wipes sweat from his forehead. I have no idea how he can be sweating in this room that is more like some kind of oversized fridge.

"Um... well, anyway. Have a good day..." The guy stumbles from the room before I can even start to answer.

Anger about myself makes me blush. "I'm sorry," I tell Lauren, not meeting her eyes.

She just shrugs. "It's his problem."

I shake my head and barely manage to suppress a sigh, glancing at the narrow aisle in front of me. "No, I should have... Guess I need..." A situation like this was the entire reason Romina and Lauren practiced steering my wheelchair with the attendant controls, but out of some reason I can't bring myself to ask for Lauren's help.

I don't want her to be my caretaker. I want her to be my friend. And much more than that.

"Come on," Lauren says, squeezing her hand on my shoulder. "The sculpture over there looks like someone covered Trump in butter. I want to marvel at that." Instead of folding out the controls behind my headrest, though, Lauren slides her left hand over my right on the armrest. Her skin is soft and feels warm compared to mine. My fingers twitch a bit as I try to relax despite the thrumming of my heart and I stare up at her, afraid she might be taken aback.

Lauren smiles, her eyes sparkling mysteriously. She moves my hand to the joystick, her fingers closing firmly over my stiff ones, and tips the stick forward gently. The wheelchair hums and rolls forward slowly and Lauren walks next to it, her hand still on mine. Together we steer the wheelchair to a sculpture that indeed bears an astonishing resemblance to the former American president, although the object label doesn't specifically say whose head is modeled.

"Hm..." Lauren says, leaning over my shoulder to look at the head. "Tempting idea indeed... What do you think?"

"Get it on video and you'll be rich, I'd say," I mumble.

"And a hero," she giggles. With her help I steer the wheelchair down the narrow aisle to the next sculpture.

The cooled-down room couldn't be large enough and have enough sculptures for my liking, so that we never have to leave it again. I love having Lauren's hand on mine and her being so close to me, so close I can smell her perfume and study her beautiful brown eyes when she bends down to look at a sculpture. I can't tell you what other people are chiseled in butter in there, because the whole time we're in this room my mind is entirely somewhere else. Much too soon, though, have we passed the last glass case in the row and are approaching the passageway leading into a wider corridor, where there's no need for Lauren to help me steer the wheelchair. I want her to continue holding my hand, but I know it'd probably be weird. She lets go just as reluctantly, brushing her fingers over my knuckles, and then increases the gap between us by half a step, to make it easier for me to avoid bumping the wheelchair into her.

I still feel the warm patch on my hand for minutes afterward.

Both Lauren and my favorite piece is a small painting of sorts. It is a rather beautiful sunset, set in – what looks like – water colors, until one watches very closely and realizes it's in fact a circular slice of sausage placed on paper that's blue on the lower half and white on the top half, with the fat soaking into the material and spreading radially out, to make it look like the rays of the sun over an ocean.

"This is um... romantic, eh?" Lauren jokes quietly. She lifts her hand up and places it on my tense neck, her warm fingers settling down casually like they belong there.

I can barely suppress a moan as a full body shudder runs through me. "Uh-huh..." I turn my head up to meet her gaze and am surprised to see the heat flashing in her eyes. Her hands are magic, the fingertips sending little thrills down my spine and I feel my entire body reacting instantly. I want her so much it's almost unbearable.

"Truly captivating..." Lauren whispers. I'm not sure if she means the art in front of us but I'm very aware that my left arm is tightening at my side and my legs tremble more than before, my shoes clanging on the footrest. My head stays turned to Lauren, thankfully. We continue staring at each other for so long that a queue is forming behind us. We are not the only people interested in seeing this small piece of art that is hanging all alone on the otherwise empty wall. So I finally break eye contact, bring myself to move the joystick to the side and then forward with all conscious effort I can muster, and we leave the area.

Although the second half of the exhibition surely is just as entertaining as everything that we have seen up to that point, I don't remember anything or anyone else than Lauren for the entire rest of it. Her walking next to me, so close I am engulfed in her cloud of perfume, her touching me from time to time, her ponytail swinging against her long neck and the occasional glimpse of her naked thighs under her skirt, it all makes me constantly teeter on the edge of madness. Just shortly prior to the end of the exhibition I roll past a rather small, somewhat hidden opening in the wall and notice a dark room behind it. I react instinctively and knock the joystick to the side. The armrests of the powerchair almost scrape the door jambs but I make it fit through with sheer luck. Lauren, who has had her hand on my shoulder, follows with a surprised gasp.

The room we enter is almost completely dark. It seems to be used as a storage for either art or cleaning utensils. In fact, I don't really care and I don't wonder about who left it open. Some way into it I turn the wheelchair around abruptly. It can go in very tight circles and Lauren obviously didn't expect that because she more or less falls into my lap with a small, surprised shriek.

"Geez, Patrick," she giggles and slightly wiggles around until she's almost straddling me in my chair. "That's—"

Lauren inhales a gasp when my right hand touches her lower back. It requires some effort but I manage to land it softly with most of my fingers splayed out. I don't pull her toward me, for one because I lack the strength and also because I'm not entirely sure she wants the same thing as I do. My heart is thrumming in my chest as I stare into her face and pray that I've not misread all the signs. She reaches with her hands to my face, framing it gently and leans closer. I don't dare to move consciously although I know it would probably be my place to close the last inch but I don't have enough faith in my body's abilities not to screw things up now. I can count Lauren's long eyelashes and smell the sweetness of her breath before her lips meet mine.

I'm not the best kisser. I wish I was but there's no way to make kissing enjoyable when one party is constantly jerking away, even if it's involuntarily. But at least I made sure that there's no spit on my face anywhere. That was my greatest concern during the entire afternoon anyway, and I think I managed okay so far. Not because I thought Lauren and I would kiss eventually, I don't think I believed I could get this lucky. No, simply because I didn't want her to have to clean saliva off me again. Although I have a small suspicion she wouldn't mind.

My head stays still for the entire time we kiss while the world seems to hold its breath with me. I feel my hand tighten on her back and my legs writhe under hers but mostly I feel the unbelievable softness of her lips against mine, and her fingers digging gently into my scalp, holding my head in place. She pulls back slowly and reluctantly, not a second too early before my face is contorting with sudden spasms and my head is thrown back against the headrest, violently.

"Oh..." Lauren watches as most of the strongest spasms pass and then presses her body closer. She places soft kisses along the side of my still mildly twitching face and my neck, making me shudder and gasp. It feels incredible. Her hands slide over both of my arms, following the bent shape of my left until she cups my quivering fist that's leaning against my chest. I squint at her in the darkness as she stills, afraid I might see repulsion in her face but there's only trembling anticipation.

"Patrick, please..." she hisses. "T-touch me..."

I stare at her. A second of inattentiveness makes my left fist slide out from under her hand and my arm jerks through the air uncontrollably. My right hand slipped from her back earlier and is writhing in my lap. I clench my teeth. I can't do it, can't she see? I might get lucky from time to time and get enough control over my right arm to move it somewhere close to where I want it to be, but it's not permanent. The brief moment of power was gone the second she kissed me, replaced by foggy arousal that makes all voluntary movement feel hundred times harder than it already is.

For some reason, though, all of that doesn't seem to matter. I don't really need to be able to touch Lauren properly to make her breath speed up and her cheeks heat. I don't know what it is that gets her going but it must be something I do because she surges in and captures my lips with hers again, moaning into my mouth. We kiss for a longer time than I've ever kissed anyone, regularly interrupted by my head jerking away. It seems like neither of us cares much about it, anymore. Lauren nips and sucks at my lower lip and draws a low groan out of me. I barely notice her taking my right hand in hers, but suddenly I can feel the perfect curves of her breasts under my fingertips and I can sense the nipples hardening beneath the light fabric of her dress as she leads my twitching fingers over them. I don't think I've ever experienced anything this beautiful.

I guess we would've gone much further than this, had a spasm not forced my head back again, pushing it into the headrest. For a few agonizing seconds I'm not looking at Lauren's blown eyes and brown strands of hair falling into her glowing face but at the ceiling of the room we're in.

"Lauren..."

Lauren's hands have lowered and she's fiddling with my belt, breathing heavily over me.

"*Lauren... stop.*"

Her fingers still although I'm not sure she understood me. "What...? Patrick, are you okay?"

I grunt and nod. "Yes, I'm... This isn't a storeroom."

Lauren stops, halfway about to kiss me again. "What?"

"This... isn't a... storeroom," I repeat, purposely slowing my speech down even more. I'm still staring at the ceiling and at what appears to be stars in the sky. For a second my mind even tricks me into believing I'm looking at the Big Dipper, which is the only constellation I'd recognize. But this is clearly stupid since it's still too early to be night.

"It's not a... what...? I don't—*Holy shit!*"

Lauren is looking up at the ceiling with me. Now that our eyes have adjusted to the dimness, we see that the room is much larger than it appeared on first glance. The ceiling is arching high over us and from above dangle what must be several hundred—

"Sausages..."

Lauren is right. Hundreds if not thousands of sausages are hanging on long threads from the ceiling, emitting a faint bluish glow. I chuckle against Lauren's side as she moves to sit sideways on my lap and leans into me to get a better look up.

"Sausages, my ass," Lauren mumbles unbelieving and laughs as well, her back shaking against my chest.

We sit like this for a while, staring at the mysterious wonder above us. A few visitors find their way through the small opening into the room, some with their phones illuminating leaflets from the museum. If we'd picked them up at the entrance we'd known there was a room showing sausages glowing in the dark. But we didn't. I'm glad we didn't but I'm also sad at the same time that I noticed at all that the room was part of the exhibition. Of course it was lucky, too, because although I very much enjoyed what we did at the conference dinner, having sex in a public exhibition room is maybe a bit too much for me.

I may be open for adventure but I'm not really sure I'll ever be ready for something like that. It becomes less enjoyable when you can't cover up and run away easily.

"Should we go?" Lauren finally whispers into my ear. We're far enough into the room that most visitors do not even spot us before they leave again. Lauren has made herself comfortable in my lap, her head resting on my shoulder and one hand splayed on my stomach. I wonder if the mild jerking my body does from time to time bothers Lauren, but it doesn't seem to be the case.

"Mmmh..." I answer and swallow against the sudden tightness in my throat. "Okay." I'd like to stop time here and never leave this room. I could keep Lauren close to me, forever, feeling her heartbeat through the layers of fabric between us, heat radiating out from her body, and could keep her sweet scent in my nose, indefinitely. But I realize we should probably leave. We both have planes to catch.

The sound of my voice attracts attention from a group of visitors who has just entered. They look over to us, some shining their phone lights into our direction. Lauren shifts but before she can sit up straight, I manage to place a kiss on her neck, making her giggle softly.

It's worth the whispers that follow us outside.

CHAPTER 12

When we exit the museum we still have another hour to go until the taxi will pick us up, and Lauren and I decide to have coffee in the museum's cafeteria. It's a glass building tacked on to the side of the concrete museum building and has a narrow door that I navigate with gritted teeth. The sleek metallic counter is very high and there's a queue of people in front of us, so I can't possibly read what is written on the chalkboards behind the counter. Lauren bends down and reads the menu to me. I appreciate the effort, but unless I ask her to negotiate with the chef about getting me a blended cake or something, I won't really eat anything here.

When it's our turn Lauren orders a milk coffee and apple pie with ice cream and whipped cream for herself, and a black coffee without sugar for me.

"Sure you don't want anything to eat?" she asks me. The young barista watches us from his position higher up, his face carefully guarded. I can tell he feels uncomfortable and if Lauren asked about blended cake, I'm pretty sure things would get complicated.

I shake my head.

I don't want to stick out again. I just want to have coffee with my date, like any ordinary person.

"Will that be all?" the guy behind the counter asks.

"Yes. A to-go cup with a straw for the black coffee, please."

The guy stares, then nods and hurriedly goes to prepare our order. Lauren rolls her eyes, turning her head so that I can see it, and pays with my money, like I asked her to do when we got in line. I'm glad she's following my wish, because there have been innumerable situations in which people paid for me, although

I didn't want them to, or despite me telling them I wanted to invite them. I know that they mean well, but the thing is, the only reason they get away with it is that I can't physically prevent them from doing it. So in my opinion it's kind of a dick move.

Lauren takes our order over to a free table, which we only reach in the narrow space in the small cafeteria because she asks a few people to pull their chairs out of the way. I try not to let it get me down and give a friendly smile to the people goggling at me as I roll past, my twitching face at their eye level.

The coffee is surprisingly good and Lauren alternates with helping me and drinking some herself. Romina showed her how to fix the cup holder at a height that makes it possible for me to reach the straw myself but Lauren doesn't use it. Because my head is not very steady I don't always manage to prevent spills when the cup is not moving in the direction that my head moves to, and that can get quite nasty with hot liquid. So I'm really glad Lauren doesn't seem to mind holding the cup for me. If anything, she seems to enjoy it.

The other thing she seems to enjoy is the pie. From time to time Lauren heaves a fork-load of the very delicious looking pie into her mouth, closing her eyes and smiling while chewing. I can barely suppress a grin seeing her like that. She's so happy and so beautiful in this moment, it just takes my breath away. The ice cream is slowly melting on the warm apples, the whipped cream is creating white swirls on the black plate, and my stomach rumbles at the sight.

Lauren giggles. "You sure you really don't want anything?" she teases.

I fidget, uncomfortable, and don't really dare to ask.

Lauren mixes a bit of the pie crust together with melted ice cream. "Would it work like this?" she asks, holding a spoon with the soft mass in front of me, grinning.

Hesitating, I eye the spoon. She's already helping me with the coffee today and letting her feed me is certainly crossing a line over to a caregiving position, in which I don't want to see her. On the other hand, she looks so enthusiastic, her eyes sparkling, I can't find it in my heart to disappoint her.

Also, the pie smells delicious.

I nod, and Lauren carefully maneuvers the spoon into my mouth. It's obvious that's the first time she's ever fed anyone, but I manage to close my mouth quickly enough to prevent anything from spilling over my lips.

"How is it?" Lauren inquires.

"Um…." I swallow slowly and then direct my eyes to the coffee. Lauren understands and quickly switches between tasks to stick the end of the straw between my lips. I flush the remnants of the cake sticking to my palate down with the coffee.

"It's good," I finally say. It tastes indeed delicious, the ice cream is cool but the dough parts that are not completely blended together with the rest are still warm. "It's got… cinnamon, right?"

Lauren nods. She goes on feeding me tiny bits of her pie mashed together with whipped cream and vanilla ice cream, and I savor every bit of it.

"I got a job offer," Lauren finally says, off-handedly. She mashes the last crumbs of pie together and finishes it.

"That's great," I say, less surprised at the fact that she got a job offer, more that it went so quickly. She had the job interview just this morning. So, did it yield better results than she had thought or did she have another interview, later? And why didn't she tell me earlier? "When? Where?"

"Um…" Lauren drinks from her coffee and offers me my straw. "Right after we talked… I told my colleagues about… you know… that I'm having trouble finding a new job and all that. And one of the guys who you met yesterday said he can help me get a job in another department. If he promotes me a bit I won't have to go through the usual hiring procedure since I will basically just switch positions within the university."

Immediately I realize that this means she won't have a real job interview. "That's good, isn't it?" I ask. Lauren doesn't look as happy as I'd expected her to be.

"Well..." she says, her eyes evading mine. "Yes and no. They're going to create a whole new research group, so it may be a chance for me to get a really good start. But... of course it's located where I'm working now."

Right. She won't be moving back home then. Well, it was a long shot anyway.

"Patrick..." Lauren sighs. "I like you..."

Oh well.

I don't think I can count how many conversations have started out like this. They always end the same. *I like you but as a friend. I like you but not like that. I like you but—* Always a 'but'.

"I really do. Back there in the room with the glowing sausages... if you hadn't stopped me..."

I stare at her, not following. Where's she going with this? Where's the 'but'?

Lauren rubs her forehead and tucks a strand of hair behind her ear, grinning sheepishly. "I'm still pissed off that wasn't a storeroom. I mean, the sausages were kinda great but..."

I can't help but chuckle when I get her meaning. Of course I've been wondering, too, how things would have developed, had we been in an undisturbed room somewhere in the museum. And I was a little disappointed as well when we noticed where we actually were.

Lauren sighs. After a while, she speaks again. "I'm not sure I'm going to take the job."

"Of course you are," I blurt out. What is she talking about?

Lauren hesitates, frowning slightly. "Pardon?"

I move my hand over to the talker's screen, inwardly cursing. "It sounds like a great offer, Lauren. Of course you'll be taking it."

Lauren still doesn't look happy. "Yes, okay, but..."

"I'm glad it wasn't a storeroom," I type. It's all in for me on this one.

Now it's Lauren who is staring at me, confused. "What?"

My hand spasms briefly because I'm trying to write too fast on the screen. I could try speaking but this would be really awkward if she didn't understand me. "I wanted it, of course, but in a way

I'm glad we didn't go that far. I like you, too. I'd like more of you. I don't know how to say this without sounding stupid but you're not a person I'd want to have sex with just this one hurried time, in a storeroom of some museum."

I think in a way I realized that just now. I want to have everything with Lauren, at the right time.

Lauren's eyes have a shimmer. "Patrick..."

With a shake of my head I shut her up, make her wait until I have finished typing. I'm surprised at her patience, really. "What does it matter that we live a bit apart? We can still text each other and skype. I'll fly over as often as I can, I promise." Lauren is still not interrupting and I hold my breath as I send the last sentence to the talker. "I guess what I really mean to say is: I want more than a one-night stand with you, Lauren."

I look up at Lauren, my heart thundering in my ears. I try to keep my cool on the outside and for once I'm not betrayed by my body. But inwardly I'm dying. What if I completely misinterpreted everything she said?

"I... me too," Lauren says abruptly and blushes immediately, turning her gaze away from me. "I want more than that, too." She smiles at me, uncharacteristically shy.

She's so damn amazing. I have no idea how I deserve her.

My body finally catches up with my inner turmoil. My knees lock, my left arm snaps to my side and my neck and parts of my face go stiff. Lauren uses her napkin to wipe at a bit of drool that escapes at the corner of my mouth. I want to dissolve with shame but her smile makes me reconsider.

Lauren takes my right hand and gently pulls it over the armrest and into her lap. We're sitting very close, so she can help me with the coffee and the food, which is the only reason she can do this without hurting me. "You'd do that?" she asks, looking into my eyes hopefully.

Because I can't speak, I blink at her, questioningly.

"Fly over, regularly?"

I groan in affirmative reply, my head jerking to the side a bit. Sure. What are a few hours in a plane compared to seeing her?

Lauren shakes her head and smiles, brushing over my knuckles with her thumb. "I'm... I'm sorry to have assumed..." she says and bites on her bottom lip. "I know so little about you. I didn't think you could... Also it's going to be so expensive!"

I'd like to shrug but that's not really happening right now. Instead I groan again. I'm sure money won't be a problem and of course I can fly over, how does she think I came here? By driving the wheelchair across states? She probably doesn't realize how much time I spend on planes. I chuckle a little and my hand twitches violently in Lauren's lap. She grips it more securely, closing her hand around my bent fingers. It feels so good, so fucking normal to be holding hands with my maybe-girlfriend in some random cafeteria, I can't quite believe my luck.

Lauren averts her eyes. "I can't pay for the plane ticket. Not very regularly, I guess."

Her salary must really be outrageously low. I know that to be the case for smaller, less endowed universities, though, so it doesn't really surprise me. It's no problem, I'll happily pay for hers.

"And even if I'd manage somehow, I don't think I'd get off from work very often. I mean, the shortest flight connections are barely less than twenty-four hours, I think."

Wait, what?

Twenty-four hours?

Where the fuck does she live?

Lauren looks at me quizzically. "What is it?"

I try pulling my hand back from her lap to access the talker but I'm not very successful. The effort causes spasms to flare up again, my left arm flapping through the air.

Lauren doesn't notice right away what is happening, that she's effectively trapping the arm I need to communicate with, but when she does she blushes deeply. "Sorry," she apologizes and helps me move my trembling hand to the screen.

"24?" I manage to type in with a bit of effort.

"Um... oh. Yes. I mean, it depends on where exactly you want to go, but fifteen to twenty-four hours are normal flight times between Australia and the US."

Australia?!

I don't need to use the talker because my facial expression says everything, I assume. Lauren's face falls immediately, her cheeks draining of color. "Yes. My current employer is in Australia. You knew that, right? I mean... Uluru? Fieldwork?" She bites on her bottom lip, her eyes desperate.

No, I didn't know shit. I thought she flew over there for a short-term trip for work. I certainly didn't think she was *living* there!

Lauren stares at me, and then laughs hollowly. "Holy shit, you didn't know..." She buries her face in her hands, shoulders sinking. "I'm so, so sorry. I thought it was clear from what I told you."

I jerk my head to the side. Nothing was clear.

Lauren groans into her hands.

Crap.

She actually lives in Australia! I can't believe my immensely bad luck. Of course I'd meet the woman of my dreams, only to realize we live twenty-four hours apart. And that's only counting flight hours, not the time that goes into preparations before I can even think of flying, the time traveling to the airport, the hours I need to account for security checkup and boarding... And while I certainly am a frequent flyer to my own dismay, I've never undertaken such a long flight. To be honest I'm not sure I can. Plus, I may be in a comfortable financial situation but I'm pretty sure that paying not only for me but also my aide's ticket to Australia and back will rip a hole even in my wallet if done too often.

We sit in silence for a while, the spasms dying down a bit.

"It won't work, will it?" Lauren asks quietly after a while. The remnants of our coffees have probably cooled down to room temperature by now.

I shrug. I can't say I'm very optimistic about a long-distance relationship to Australia. It probably means we won't meet more often than once or twice a year.

"I thought so, too," Lauren says once I have communicated that through the talker. Still, her eyes have never looked so sad. "I'm sorry."

"It's not your fault." It's just bad luck I guess. My bad luck. How could I ever think it would be different? "I'll need a minute," I say finally after a pause, my throat tight.

Lauren looks at me and seems to pull herself together. She gestures with her hand. "Do you need me to—?"

I shake my head resolutely, almost angrily. "Meet you outside in ten?"

I push against the joystick to make the wheelchair jolt backward and then swing around to face the exit. I make my way out, grunting impatiently at those people who sit in my way and bellowing at a few slower ones to move using my own voice, not caring to modulate the volume correctly. I barely notice most customers' panicked scramble as they clear the space or the wide-eyed stares as I roll past. When I near the exit a guy jumps up from his seat to hold the door open for me and I steer past him without so much as a muttered thanks.

Lauren joins me a while later. She has picked up her suitcase from the museum's lockers and her eyes are a bit red but she seems to have recovered. She even smiles a little as she sees me, although it vanishes quickly again. "You traumatized a few people in there," she says quietly. "I think that's the last time they leave their bags on the floor."

Guiltily, I glance back at the cafeteria entrance. Shit, I didn't intend to be that nasty. I guess I can be unbearable when I'm in a bad mood.

"I told them you were mad because the museum wouldn't sell you Trump's head in butter."

Disbelieving, I chuckle. "You didn't!"

Lauren's laugh is the most beautiful thing and I can't help but join in. Lauren sits down next to me on one of the boulders marking the entrance to the cafeteria, and rolls the suitcase to her other side. "The taxi won't come for another ten minutes…" she informs me.

I know. "I called it to come earlier if possible." Well, Romina did, after I asked her to. Among other things.

"Oh..." Lauren nods and looks down at her shoes, clearly disappointed I have cut down on our last remaining minutes together. It gives me a stab in the heart to see it, but it was necessary to do.

We don't wait long for the taxi to arrive. The driver is the same guy as before. I assume there aren't many taxis of that sort around even in this big city. Lauren helps me get settled while the taxi driver is as gloriously unhelpful as before, and then we're off to the airport.

The drive is silent for most parts. Lauren and the driver are sitting in the front and I'm sitting in my wheelchair in the back. I can only see part of Lauren's face and her hair from behind because she doesn't turn around to me this time. Traffic is smooth and we're getting close to the airport much faster than anticipated.

"Can you stop here for a second?" Lauren suddenly asks the driver about halfway between the museum and the airport. He gives her an annoyed look but pulls over at the next possibility.

"What's wrong now?" the driver asks Lauren as she exits the car. He's leaning over the middle console to look at her as she jumps out.

"Nothing," Lauren quickly says and pulls open the sliding doors to the back. I watch her duck inside and squeeze through to me, a grin on her lips.

"There's no space for two people back there," the taxi driver says impatiently. He has turned around and is frowning at us in the back.

He's right, in fact, because the taxi itself isn't spacious and the powerchair takes up most of the space. I think there's a seat folded down on one side but it's exactly where I'm parked.

"Sure there is," Lauren says and sits on my lap sideways with one arm around my neck. She straightens her dress and turns to look at the driver. "What are you waiting for?"

The taxi driver stares. "This is against safety regulations," he complains, not moving a finger to pull into traffic. "I can't do this."

Lauren tightens her hold around me. "Oh come on…"

"Nope."

It doesn't sound like there's anything that may change his mind and Lauren sighs, defeated. It shakes something awake in me, seeing her like this. In a few minutes we'll depart, maybe forever, and Lauren is right: we shouldn't spend the remaining time quiet and sitting apart from each other in a taxi, just because this guy can't look the other way for once. I'm pretty sure he wouldn't care if we were able-bodied customers making out in the back of his car. No, this won't happen, not if I can prevent it. "I need her to…" I say, slowly and with the greatest effort, to make Lauren understand every word. It is hard, I can barely get a grip on myself with her sitting in my lap, again so wonderfully close to me it's making me dizzy.

"I need to make sure that…?" Lauren repeats what I've said, looking at me questioningly. The taxi driver stares at me with wide eyes while I try to get my jaw and tongue to cooperate enough to continue talking.

"That I'm not getting sick," I finally manage to say. "I don't take sitting in the back very well."

Lauren relays word-by-word. The taxi driver frowns and looks like he's failing at trying to stay calm. "Tell him, he's very welcome to sit in the front," he snaps nastily.

I'm almost sure he knows that's not an option for me. I'm not so sure he knows I can hear and understand him perfectly, though.

"Thing is, I won't drive with you two like this."

Lauren freezes and sits up. She slowly tilts her head, a small smile playing around her lips. Thank god, she caught on to what I was trying to do. "Did you just say you're refusing to transport a severely disabled man in your accessible car?"

Go, Lauren.

The taxi driver swallows.

"I'm sure you didn't say that, am I right?" Lauren asks in a dangerously sweet voice. "Patrick, did you hear this guy saying he won't take you in his taxi?"

Trying to evade the gaze of the taxi driver boring into us, I groan something unintelligible on purpose. I'm sure he is entitled to deny service to anyone, but he knows he'll not be the hero of this tale if word gets out about the condition of his client.

The face of the taxi driver grows red with anger and he opens and closes his mouth a few times. "Fine," he hisses finally. "Is he going to vomit?"

I try shaking my head but end up bumping it into the headrest with a muffled grunt. Ah well, it's all the same.

"I don't think he will. If you drive carefully," Lauren says smugly and I feel a grin tug at my lips.

During the last few days, I got to know Lauren as a determined person, but I guess even I am surprised by her persistence. There is still so much to explore about Lauren, I realize, so much I don't know about her.

The taxi driver scowls at Lauren but then he abruptly turns back to look out the front. The motor howls, the van bumps down the sidewalk and we're back on the road. The furrowed eyebrows of the pissed-off taxi driver track us in the rearview mirror.

Lauren turns to me, smiling, and her face lowers to mine. "That was amazing, Patrick," she whispers.

I smile and dip my head to her, giving the compliment back.

"Is he going to kiss me?" Lauren whispers, imitating the way the taxi driver talked over me instead of to me.

He may be damned if he doesn't.

I don't say that, though, because it would take too long and we don't have time for unimportant things. I lean forward a fraction, concentrating on the task ahead with my right hand braced on the armrest, and seal our lips together.

CHAPTER 13

"Is Romina waiting inside?"

I nod.

The second part of the taxi drive to the airport was even shorter than the first half, at least in my memory. The city was flying by outside the windows as Lauren's hands were roaming over my body, her fingertips gliding over twitching muscles and writhing limbs, caressing every inch she could reach with a tender determination that made hot waves of pleasure run through me. The driver's incredulous stare in the rearview mirror couldn't stop us, in fact we barely noticed it. For us, there was no one present in the car other than Lauren and me, and we could have been driving through any country at any time, it didn't matter. Her lips were sweet and warm on mine and her tongue carefully exploring, tentatively licking into my mouth. She tasted better than anything I've ever had and I couldn't get enough of her, praying to my body to keep behaving the way it did, with only minor tremors traveling through it that neither of us really took notice of.

I never wanted it to stop. I wanted the taxi to drive rounds through the city and never come to its destination, caught in an endless loop of space and time, with Lauren in my lap.

But of course, it did eventually end and because traffic was still less congested than expected, we arrived a little earlier than we'd thought, even though we'd stopped along the way.

Lauren paid with my money and the disgruntled look partly vanished from the driver's face when her tip almost doubled the taxi fare. This time, he even demeaned himself enough to help her detach the straps fixing the wheelchair to the car floor. Lauren then used the attendant controls to steer my chair down the ramp backwards, like a pro.

Now, Lauren is standing next to me by the road while people stream around us. She clutches the handle of her red suitcase closely to herself. I don't have my suitcase with me because Romina is taking care of my luggage, as always.

Lauren stares at the rotating doors of the entrance to the terminal and I can tell she's nervous to say goodbye. She has to catch a bus to the international terminal and there's no real point for her to go inside the building with me. She turns around to me. "We will try to stay in contact, won't we?" she asks.

I nod. We can always try, can't we?

"Okay, cool..."

It's now or never. I've made my decision. I've made it long before, actually. Maybe already when Lauren showed up at the speaker's table after my talk.

"Would you... um... help me find Romina?" I ask her and jerk my head to the terminal building. Behind the glass wall, people with their luggage are bustling around, families and business travelers, flight assistants and airport workers. At regular intervals announcements over the speakers can be heard, slightly muffled. It's not that far-fetched to ask for help finding someone in these conditions, especially when your line of sight is at most people's chest height.

Lauren's head flies up and she beams, something bright glowing in her eyes. "Yes, of course." Luckily, she's equally eager to prolong the time with me until we have to part. Her flight is in a couple of hours, so she has time for that, too.

That makes it easy.

To be honest, I could find Romina on my own, without major problems. The airport is fully accessible even to me and I know pretty much exactly where she'll be, because we always have meeting points for cases like this. But I have other plans and they require Lauren to stay with me for a little while longer.

We enter through the wide wheelchair entrance to the right of the rotating doors after I bump the front part of my right armrest against the large button that opens the automatic door.

"Did you agree upon a meeting point?" Lauren asks as we're standing in the middle of the foyer.

Knowing Lauren doesn't expect me to give a more detailed explanation, I nod, and take a few seconds to orient myself. I'm more familiar with some of the international airports than the supermarket in the town where I live. Granted, that might have to do a lot more with the fact that I almost never go grocery shopping and less to do with me being a frequent flyer, but it's still true.

"Follow me."

Slowly, we make our way through the crowd of people and into one of the large elevators that is already waiting. We ride up to the waiting area with shops and restaurants and I lead the way to cross through to the side of the building facing the runway, pretending I'm looking out for signs and directions although I pretty well know where we're going.

"Patrick…" Lauren's footsteps stop shortly before resuming following me. By now, we've managed to leave the crowd behind and are moving down a clean, empty corridor.

"Mmmh…?" Deliberately, I tip the joystick a little further forward, listening to Lauren's steps quickening behind me.

"Where are we going?" she calls to my back. "Are you sure—"

We round a corner and stop short in front of two large sliding doors with milky glass panes and golden decorations painted on.

"Hello ma'am, sir. What can I do for you?"

The young guy in a spotless black suit standing right behind a small counter on the side and smiling at us in a practiced way doesn't look familiar to me. Damn, why do they always change out personnel so quickly?

The guy's smile doesn't waver the slightest when a small groan escapes me.

"Are you members?"

I want to nod but my neck has other plans unfortunately. My head cranes back and a couple of grimaces flit over my face.

"Can I see your membership cards, please?" The guy addresses

Lauren when I don't seem to react. "Ma'am?"

"Um…" Lauren bows down to me, slightly worried. "This looks like a business lounge or something, Patrick. I think we should just—"

Frustrated with my body, I grunt something and force the knuckles of my right hand to lean against the screen. I've just started the slow process of typing when a second, middle-aged man comes through the door behind the counter and relief washes over me.

Immediately when he sees us, a smile spreads on his round face. "Ah, Mr. Hallman! We've been awaiting you."

"Suresh… hi…" I don't think I've ever felt more grateful for being the most recognizable guy in an airport lounge.

Suresh comes around the counter, squeezes my upper right arm and cups my right fist on the joystick in a sort-of handshake. Although it surprises me, I certainly like it more than people standing around awkwardly with no clue what to do.

"Ah…" Suresh turns to Lauren, smiling at her warmly as well. "Well, well… Who is the beautiful lady?" he asks brightly and offers his hand to Lauren.

"Um… Lauren Brooks," Lauren says, shaking his hand and throwing confused looks to me.

"It is a pleasure to meet you, Miss Brooks." Suresh gesticulates to the sliding doors. "Please, please, follow me through here. Would you like something to drink, Miss Brooks? Champagne perhaps?"

"Um…"

"Alex, go and fetch two glasses of our best, would you? And one straw."

"Oh… um… of course." The young guy startles, his gaze flits over to me before he vanishes behind the door at his back while we follow Suresh into the lounge.

It's not the largest lounge in this airport, nor does it have the best view or the best drinks. The better lounges are located after security. But this one is still rather convenient if you have a meeting scheduled directly after arrival, or simply need an undisturbed place in the city. Right now there are not many people present. There's an older guy in a corner in a red plush chair, reading a newspaper and checking his watch every few seconds, apparently waiting for someone. And at a table in the back there's Romina, in front of a glass of champagne.

"I already checked our luggage," she says in lieu of greeting when we approach.

"Thanks," I say. I know from experience with this airport that I can stay in my powerchair until shortly before boarding, which is a blessing. There's nothing worse than being forced into an airport wheelchair that doesn't provide nearly enough support for me. I always feel like I'm falling out every time even moderate spasms grip my body or simply when I go around a corner, because the seat is not molded to fit my crooked body. Plus, I can't steer those manual chairs myself and even if I don't fall out, I tend to slide into uncomfortable positions that make it hard to breathe. So yes, as much as I despise my own chair at times, I know that in reality it's one of the most valuable things I own.

I maneuver the wheelchair around the last table and arrive at Romina's place. Suresh has made sure to move all chairs out of my way but of course he can't make the tables vanish. "Thanks, Suresh."

Suresh bows a little. "If you need anything you only need to ask, Mr. Hallman. Your drinks will be with you in no time."

I smile at him and he leaves. Lauren sits across from me, hesitantly. "Fancy lounge..." she begins and frowns at me. "Isn't your flight leaving soon?"

I ignore her for now and turn my head slightly to look at Romina. She nods, answering my unspoken question, which makes me feel lighter immediately. Everything is set.

"We'll have to make this quick," I say to Lauren and Romina relays. I would have tried earlier to explain to Lauren what I have in mind, but there just wasn't enough time to communicate all this using the talker while we were traveling in the taxi. Or better, I didn't want to make time for it, while we had other, more pleasurable things to do.

"You need a job, Lauren, right? One that isn't in Australia," I add with a small smirk and Lauren nods slowly, still frowning.

Our drinks arrive but no one notices. Lauren is staring at me, trying to parse the words while I work through my little speech, too impatient to wait for Romina to relay them.

"The company I'm associated with plans to start a new project, together with Colin Curtbell's institute. It could potentially be interesting to you. He's currently in search of someone to work on this with him and I'm sure he'd be thrilled to take you on." He better be, I let him know I send Lauren with high regard. Of course, he's also aware that I'm stupidly in love with the woman I suggested works with us, so in his eyes that may cloud my judgment.

It doesn't, I'm very sure of it. Lauren is a perfect candidate.

I tell Lauren very briefly what the project will be about. "It's in the UK but since you'll work closely with us, you'd be in the US more often than in the UK. I can promise you that," I close.

Lauren has listened closely, her breath almost held.

"Would you be interested in that position, theoretically?" I ask, a little hesitant when Lauren doesn't react.

With a bit of delay, Lauren blinks and then nods, quickly, as if I could retract that offer otherwise. "Of course, Patrick. That sounds... that sounds great! How—"

"Excellent," I interrupt her because we don't have much time left. I turn to my aide. "Romina? Did Colin—"

"He's already here," Romina says and places a tablet on the table in front of us and opens the video chat. Colin grins and waves at us from what looks like a seat in a crowded airport terminal, close to the gates. This airport, to be precise. His plane will leave for the UK in a few minutes. "Good to see you, Patrick! Miss Brooks. Shall we begin with the interview?"

"Um..." Lauren looks from me to the tablet, alarmed. I can see her tensing up the second Colin addresses her and mentions the nature of the conversation.

I knew that surprising Lauren with a last-minute job interview wasn't the most sensible idea, but Colin has to present possible additions to his group to his faculty tomorrow, which is why time was of the utmost importance for my plan to work. I called Romina from outside the museum and instructed her to make a couple of phone calls; one to Colin, to ask him to consider taking Lauren on as a new addition to his team, and one with my brother, to clear things about the new project. I also asked Romina to set up this video call. If Lauren secures this job position, it'll be almost entirely like she moved back to where she grew up, and we could see each other a hundred times more often than if she stayed in Australia.

"Uh..." Lauren looks like she lost a bit of color, her eyes widening. "Okay..."

I didn't tell Colin about Lauren's issues. There wasn't enough time and I felt like it wasn't my place to tell. I had hoped that my presence and the fact that the interview was via video call would help calm her nerves, but that doesn't seem to be the case. Lauren stares at the screen, practically frozen. To my dismay, she is sitting too far away for me to have any hopes to touch her and reassure her, so I smile and attempt to nod at her encouragingly.

Colin chuckles a little and adjusts his screen. "You seem to have recovered much better from last night than I have, Miss Brooks," he says in a conversational tone. "My headache could kill a bear," he groans.

Finally, Lauren seems to wake up from the initial shock. She clears her throat. "Oh yeah, that was probably one Pisco Sour too many," she points out and Colin laughs, then stops himself with another groan.

I need not have worried. Over the last few days, I got to know Colin as an emotionally intelligent, sensible man, and he instinctively handles the situation perfectly. After just a few light jokes, Lauren is reminded that she sang Eye of the Tiger with the guy who is interviewing her, and that certainly does the trick. She relaxes and starts being her witty, confident self.

"Patrick has sent me a few notes on your CV..." Colin goes on, scrolling through something on his phone.

"He has?" Lauren looks at me, puzzled, and I shrug. Whoever my brother instructed with researching personal information about Lauren, I'm mildly impressed by the quick and thorough work, and I make a mental note to ask who he asked to do it.

"I'm afraid boarding is going to close soon," Colin remarks with an apologetic expression, facing the screen again. "So, this job interview will have to be short now, but we can have a much longer chat next week."

Lauren freezes slightly at another mention of the job interview, but she pulls herself together remarkably. "Okay... That's fine with me."

The interview is short as expected and, for most parts, goes smoothly. As in conversations with me, Colin proves to be a good listener and grants Lauren time to gather her thoughts, waiting for her to arrive at a point she wants to make, even if she takes a bit of a detour at the beginning as her nerves show. But with time, she visibly relaxes again and it soon becomes clear that the two get along splendidly. Who could be intimidated by Colin, anyway, when his broad face is constantly smiling from the screen?

In the end both joke about going for drinks again, when we all meet in the UK upon the start of the project.

"Awesome," Colin says, reaching for his coat on the seat next to him. "I have to go. I think we'll settle details of the project with Patrick within the next few days, and we can talk again then. You don't need to make a decision right now, but if you are interested in general, I'll bring you up as a possible candidate with the board."

"That sounds great. Thank you so much, Mr. Curtbell, I'm definitely very much interested," Lauren says, grinning, her eyes sparkling again with life. The sight makes me incredibly happy.

"Great. And please call me Colin again," Colin says, waving a hand. "The formal part is over, isn't it?"

"Right..." Lauren beams. "Thanks, Colin."

"I wish you a good flight home, Lauren. And Patrick, let's

chat as soon as possible, alright? And let me know about the scholarship program you're planning. Could be interesting for Lauren, too."

I grunt and Romina steps behind Lauren, giving Colin a thumbs up from me. Then we have to part from Colin as he stands in line to board the plane.

"Whew..." Lauren leans back in her chair and blows a strand of hair out of her face. "That was quick," she says, her eyes turned down.

"You did well," I say.

Lauren tucks the strand of hair behind her ear and looks up at me, her cheeks a little rosy. "Did I?"

I nod, which makes her grin.

"Did you come up with all that just an hour ago?" she asks me after a while.

"We had planned for a joint project all along, but I, and mostly Romina, may have enforced things a little." I catch Romina's gaze at that, who shrugs and grins, not letting anything on. It was probably the easier task to sway Colin. A bigger challenge would have been convincing my brother, who didn't have a clue about Colin and what we've discussed the other night. But as I know my brother, Romina probably only had to mention Lauren's name and that this project was necessary to bring Lauren and me within some realistic dating distance, and he'd have approved of it.

"What's that scholarship program Colin mentioned?"

I promise to tell her later, especially since it's still more fiction than reality. Hebert didn't express much enthusiasm for financing young researchers on high-risk projects when I first talked to him about it, but I seem to be gaining ground with the other members of the committee. Initially it was de Jong who pushed me to pursue this further, but the more I talked to people about it, the more I convinced myself that it's in fact a really good idea.

Lauren doesn't have to worry about financial details for the first years of her project, though. We'll figure something out between Colin and myself.

"Then we'll work together soon, huh?" Lauren looks at me, happily. "That's so cool! Thank you so much, you two, you are both geniuses!" She beams at Romina, who blushes a little and smiles.

I chuckle. "Yeah. It may still be a few months until the project starts. And as for working together... I can't promise to be involved too much." These days I don't really do much hands-on work. "But someone from the company will be. And we'll make sure your presence is required at our place during much of the time."

"Awesome!"

Lauren looks like only Romina's presence prevents her from throwing herself at me. Instead, she grabs her glass of champagne. "Cheers! To a new job opportunity that isn't 24 flight hours away!"

Romina lifts my glass to meet Lauren's and I sip a little champagne while Lauren pours hers down. "Thanks for everything... Patrick," she says as she places her empty glass down, her eyes resting on me.

I smile back at her, my stomach making tiny flips of joy. If all goes as I hope, she'll practically move back and we'll be able to see each other regularly. For a second, I allow myself to start dreaming about the things we will do. We can go have lunch together and after work we can do those ordinary things that people do in their free time, like going to the cinema or bowling. We'll be colleagues but not directly involved in each other's work, so that won't make things awkward, I hope. We can go to a museum again, to the theater, have breakfast together on weekends... There are endless possibilities ahead of us and I can hardly wait for it to start. It's still a few months until things will be settled, though, and I already feel impatient now.

It isn't long until Romina announces it's time for us to leave. Lauren takes the handle of her suitcase in hand and we exit, Suresh and Alex escorting us out with lots of well-wishes. I have to promise them I'll come back whenever I stay in the city next time.

The dreaded entrance to the security line that can only be crossed by passengers with a domestic flight ticket arrives much too early. The wheelchair's wheels squeak as I make it turn around to face Lauren. In the corner of my eyes I can see that Romina gives us space, chatting up the security personnel guarding the area.

"I'll miss you," I say to Lauren before I grow too anxious to say it, inwardly crossing my fingers she'll understand me.

Lauren smiles, her eyes glistening a bit. "Me too," she says. She watches my right arm slip from the armrest and the fingers twitch a bit in my lap, before taking my hand in hers, squeezing lightly. I can't believe how well she can gauge what I'd like to do even if my body doesn't always let me. "We'll video chat, okay?"

I nod, my legs quivering as I try to squeeze her hand back. "I can't wait," I say out loud what's on my mind. "I really..." I wait for a facial spasm to pass before going on, "...want to see you again."

"We'll see each other again."

It's an actual effort to suppress a sigh. "If only I could make you stay now..." I've done what I could, though. There's no way to make her stay here right now, I know that. And it's not her fault, either. It will be good for her career to finish up with what she has started in Australia, too, before she'll move on to other things.

Lauren shakes her head with her lips pressed together and I'm left wondering if she understood me when she bends down and kisses me softly on the lips, shortly before my head jerks away.

"I'd stay if I could," she whispers. "I like you a lot, Patrick." She replaces my hand on the joystick and gently thumbs away some wetness under my left eye. My face is hot but somehow I'm not embarrassed because I can see Lauren is fighting tears, too.

"Give my greetings to Uluru," I say slowly, already moving the wheelchair around toward the entrance to security, where Romina is waiting.

"Maybe you can give them yourself," Lauren says. She keeps

standing with her suitcase, watching me wheel away. "Not the way you'd prefer, but still......"

I grimace but yes, she's right. "Maybe."

She lifts her hand and waves at me, and I swivel the chair around to her fully again and lift a finger from the armrest, my left arm snapping to my chest and my face contorting again. Well, what a wonderful last image of me.

Lauren smiles, though, and then she's swallowed by the crowd and I concentrate on steering the wheelchair through the narrow gap to the short line of first and business class security, Romina following me. A middle-aged man in an airport uniform is already waiting at the front of the line and waving at me with a pair of plastic gloves in his hands. I sigh but I manage to give him a friendly nod.

It's only a few months, not even half a year. And maybe, if I can make myself go through with it and board a plane to freaking Australia in the course of it, it may be even shorter than that. I'm already dreading the journey, but I know one thing for sure:

It will be worth it.

EPILOGUE

The hotel room is neat and spacious but impersonal like the many others I've been in. From my position I can see the orange wall in front of me and the large windows that would give a beautiful view over the twinkling lights on the coast during nighttime were it not for the curtains drawn shut. I'm propped up against a stack of pillows in my back. The hotel room's mattress is soft; I feel like I'm sinking deeper into it with every unwanted quiver of my body. Of course there aren't any grab bars within my reach, and strong spasms could possibly tip me over, but I'll have to trust Romina's skill with the pillows. The faint nudge in my lower back tells me she squeezed some against my side as well as behind my back, so in theory I should be fine. My legs are supported by pillows and my hands are twitching on top of the blanket, restlessly. The blanket is not really necessary due to the mild temperatures, but I asked Romina for it, after she had undressed me and before she left to explore the hotel bar.

The last days have been wonderful, relaxed and light, full of joyful conversation with Lauren and rounds of Australian wine. They have been everything I imagined during the six weeks that we were separated after the conference. We've spent most of our time together, visiting museums or driving around with the van that I rented, at first always accompanied by Romina but more and more often just Lauren and me. Lauren showed me the places where she works, the lab and the offices, and we've gone out with her colleagues a few times. I met Paige and Lu again, which was awesome, and though it was awkward with the others at the beginning, like usual when I meet new people, the staring subsided eventually. Already then I was glad I went through it all to come here.

The door to Romina's room, which is adjacent to mine, opens and Lauren steps inside. She's wearing a rose dressing gown, the silk flowing around her beautifully shaped body like water. Her dark brown hair is tied into a bun on top of her head, but a strand of hair has escaped, curling down her long neck.

"You're—" I start saying but my throat is clogged and only wet gurgling comes out. I cough weakly, my right fist pushing into the thick mattress repeatedly. "You look gorgeous," I croak then. It comes out alright; I'm having a good day speech-wise and I squint up at Lauren, hoping she understood me.

Lauren has become better at understanding me during recent weeks as we spoke via phone or video chat, although she's of course nowhere nearly as good at it as Romina or my brother. That takes more time. But she's come a long way already and I had to use the talker far less than expected in the last days.

The situation now is a slightly different one, though. It's difficult for me to use the talker while in bed and it would definitely be in the way of certain activities. The tablet is on the nightstand to my right and if need be I could use it, provided Lauren holds it in the right position for me. But other than that I have to make myself understood without my technical aides. Since arousal worsens my spasms tenfold and that directly affects my speech, it's a game I'm bound to lose.

Just as I feared, Lauren hesitates. But then she looks up and a broad smile splits her face. "Thanks," she says and doesn't break eye contact. "But really it's thanks to Romina's shower though. I think I still may have sand in my ear." She sticks a finger into her left ear and wiggles it around, making a funny face at the same time.

I can't help but let out a wheezing laugh. Among all women I've ever slept with, or ever aspired to sleep with, Lauren is easily the most beautiful. But definitely no one I ever met was this sexy while cleaning out their ear canals. It's ridiculous, really.

"What?" Lauren says, giggling too. "We spent almost all day at the coast and the wind was blowing!"

That's true, I have to give her that.

Lauren's eyes find mine and she blushes.

"Come here," I say softly to Lauren and nod with my head to the space next to me in bed.

We've had the heavier conversations before, via skype or email. I've heard from her own mouth that Lauren's into me, and into every part of my disability, although she can't explain why either. We've settled for not trying to find an explanation and decided to explore the physical parts when I come visit. I've tried to prepare her for everything, while knowing it is literally impossible.

I must say, so far, she's taken everything remarkably in stride.

Lauren pads closer, the door falling shut behind her. "Thank god," she sighs as she plops down on the mattress. "I'm absolutely shattered." The mattress depresses slightly more when she leans down for a quick kiss. Her lips taste sweet and are as soft as ever, her smell is familiar and I feel the faint tremble in her body as our lips connect, indicating that she isn't as collected as she seems on the outside.

She's practically vibrating with desire. And so am I.

By chance, my right hand is close to Lauren's where she braces herself on the mattress, and I manage to lean it a bit to the side, my knuckles slowly grazing up the inner side of her wrist. Lauren shudders and exhales over me, her eyes fluttering close for a moment. I see goosebumps form on her arm.

"Come under the covers?" I suggest. She's done that during the first days after my arrival, after Romina had finished preparing me for sleep. Each night, Lauren slipped into bed next to me, in her nightdress, and propped her head on my chest, her body so close I could feel her warmth along mine. Her hands played with mine and we talked in low voices about the day and what lies ahead. It was wonderful. Since I can't visit her at her apartment because it isn't accessible at all, this has been the only chance for us to be truly alone together.

"I'm going to fall asleep if I lie down now," Lauren says, yawning. Then she leans down to me, hesitates, and whispers into my ear: "Please undress me, Patrick." Her breath is warm.

"I'd like to get naked for you."

I had told Lauren I'm okay with taking it slow. That we wouldn't need to do anything other than cuddling during my visit. I had given Lauren all the ways out that I can think of, I must admit, out of worry of pressuring her into something she couldn't handle, then. Or ever. If she needed to stop, she knew I was absolutely fine with it.

I guess that's proof of how out of my mind I was with fear she could hate what she sees. Because of course I wanted things to not go slow at all.

And luckily she doesn't, either.

My cheeks heat and I smile, thinking back to the first time Lauren asked me to undress her, in this hotel room. I had been confused, not sure I was understanding her right, my left arm twitching at my side like it wanted to prove my point. I can't take my own clothes off, there's literally no way I could do what she desired me to do.

But it didn't take me long to notice that this is completely beside the point.

Lauren pushes off the mattress and walks back a few steps until she's in plain view a few feet from my position in the bed, a glint in her eyes. She pauses, watching me like she's waiting for something and I nod.

"Belt..." I whisper, my throat suddenly raw. As Lauren's hands move, I imagine myself as the one beginning to loosen the knot around her belt.

A spasm cranks my head back and I feel my face contorting nastily. The knowledge of how ridiculous I must look makes me cringe for a second. The blanket is covering most parts of my body and I suddenly feel very grateful for it. When Lauren comes back into view, her hands have settled on the silken band around her waist, patiently waiting for my attention to return to her. She blinks when our eyes meet and smiles sheepishly like a child caught with its hands in the cookie jar. The silk slides apart without sound as Lauren finally opens the belt around the dressing gown. I catch a glimpse of her dark, almost black, wiry pubic hair between her legs. Then the cloth falls back into place, leaving many details to imagination but still not covering enough.

That thought is driving me literally crazy. I know her perfect body in all its entire nakedness, I can almost feel her unblemished skin and the round curves against my bent bones. I want her so much, it's overwhelming and for a second I forget to breathe. I swallow and gasp for air, my breath irregular and loud now, with an ugly, embarrassing rattle in the back of my throat. My eyes close to give me space to get some control but it doesn't seem to help. The room feels like it's turning around itself, just like the kitchen in the museum we visited on our first date, right after the conference where we met.

"Mrr... Slww..." I stop myself, realizing my throat is not cooperating at all. There's too much saliva and I can't seem to be able to convince myself to swallow again, my mouth rapidly filling with liquid that is threatening to clog my airways. I start having trouble breathing and I'm only seconds away from panicking.

Shit, shit, shit.

"Hey..." Lauren is somewhere over me, adjusting the pillows in my back and tipping my head forward gently until my chin almost touches my chest, a method she has learned from Romina. "Better?" she whispers.

I manage to swallow and immediately don't feel like I'm drowning anymore. The heat of shame creeps into my face. That's how fast everything goes down the drain, I'm afraid. My body goes into overdrive and I lose all basic command over it, even the shreds that usually remain to me.

Lauren vanishes from my field of vision and despite knowing better, I refuse to give up to the still ongoing spasms, the muscles in my chest tightening. My jaw hurts with the force I'm trying to make it behave and squeeze out words of apology, with little success. "Hnghh..." My lungs start burning again, this time from the fast, shallow gasps with which I suck in air between trying to talk.

"Patrick."

With effort I manage to turn my attention away from my rebellious body and follow the sound, lifting my head up a bit. Lauren is standing a few steps away, her chest heaving. There're beads of sweat forming on the uncovered parts of her body, her chest and arms and upper lip, glistening like small diamonds on her skin. She licks her lips and her hands slowly reach up into her hair, watching me with a questioning look. When I don't object, she loosens the band that keeps her hair together and the dark locks fall around her face to her shoulders, making her look even more stunning than before.

"Should I go on?" Lauren asks.

Lauren's distraction is working wonders and my chest muscles finally loosen up. I hum, relieved, and jerk my head into a nod. My left arm is still twitching back and forth at my side, and my right hand convulses into the sheets forcefully. But as I watch Lauren, it's easy to imagine how it must be to touch her dressing gown, feel the cool material run through my fingers before sliding it down her shoulders slowly, revealing all of her. The effect is amazing and I notice myself grow hard just looking at Lauren standing still in front of me, wondering if she knows.

"Please," I rasp. I'm all hers now. "Let me..."

Lauren's breath is quickening and she still hasn't moved, her eyes darker and full of lust as she looks at me. She knows perfectly well what she's doing to me. My legs tremble without pause under the blanket, pressed together at the knees, their thin, sharp contours visible through the fabric. For a short moment I feel uncomfortable being stared at but mostly it arouses me immensely. I remember that feeling from the very first time when we met and I first experienced I had this effect on her, that I could make her crazy just by moving an arm or trying to speak in the way that I do, and it is the same now. I've never experienced this with anyone else but Lauren. My heart drums like crazy in my chest and sweat collects on my skin. I'm not usually in a position like this, as the one giving pleasure as much as receiving it.

Then Lauren shifts and the cloth glides from her shoulders, pooling around her naked feet, granting me full view of her breasts. I can't see much of her body below that, I've slipped further down from the slightly reclined position I'm sitting in, but that doesn't matter. Her breasts are as perfect as I ever could have imagined breasts to be, round, perking up despite the heat, the nipples dark and hard.

My breath catches in my throat.

"Do you like that?" Lauren asks, though I think it must be rhetorical. She knows I love her body.

My left arm has lifted, hovering somewhere over my head and I try to ignore it. "A lot," I manage finally, attempting a wry grin while my right knee is jerking up and down under the covers.

It feels like a victory when Lauren blushes. Only because she knows I'm enjoying her show doesn't mean I can't tell her and revel in her reaction.

Lauren's light footfalls advance again. I watch her over the outline of my contracted, thin legs and my slightly protruding belly, visible under the thin blanket. She smiles, her eyes full of fire.

The first time we've been intimate I almost chickened out. Despite everything, despite every word and every action of Lauren that showed me crystal clear that she wants me, I still feared she may change her mind once she's seen the whole of me. I know it was foolish, but somehow my brain told me that she just hadn't caught on yet, that once she would see me completely naked and uncovered, she may realize the truth and notice she's in bed with a severely disabled person.

Now I think she knows the truth perfectly well. And she enjoys it.

Lauren climbs into bed and slowly crawls over to me, never breaking eye contact. At a nod of my head, she lifts the blanket up over my feet. Her hand lands warm on my naked, turned-in right foot, her fingers folding around the ankle, just staying there. She breathes heavily, watching a small tremor run up my legs.

Then the blanket slides further up, slipping over my knees. Lauren's fingers follow up my shins, then stop. "The pillow..." Lauren begins quietly and lets the sentence trail off. She moves her hand to the rubber foam pillow under my knees, not touching it. She didn't ask about it before and I don't know why I never told her. I guess with so many more pressing matters to get off my chest it just went down in the awkwardness of cripple pre-sex talk. And then I forgot about it.

"I need..." I know there's no shame in it but somehow it's difficult to explain it to her. "Can't..." I jerk my head to my legs and hope Lauren knows I'd be more eloquent if she weren't naked and my body were not currently still wrecked with minor spasms.

"You can't... um... oh. You can't straighten your legs?"

I nod, glad that I got through to her somehow.

Lauren captures my writhing hand and if she has more questions she doesn't ask them. After a while, she lifts the blanket further off me. Her eyes follow the jerky movement as this causes one leg to go into spasm, the knee locking and the muscle in my thigh twitching as it shifts to fold over the other. Lauren lets her hand trail over my shin and cups my knobby knee, moaning a bit as it lifts off against the weight of her hand, her eyelashes fluttering as she looks at me.

"Is this okay?"

I force my right hand to relax into the sheets, my left arm thudding against my chest, and blink. Yes.

Lauren lets her hand wander further up and traces the outline of the flexing muscle in my unnaturally small thigh.

She hasn't removed the blanket from my waist area and she doesn't, not yet. She pulls the top of the blanket down over my upper body, her fingers moving over my stomach, skirting around my belly button. My body jolts at each touch, wicked spasms rippling through it but I don't tell her to stop. My upper body is sliding a bit sideways, the support of the pillows not enough to hold me up against the shaking. Lauren props me up again, taking her time to gently fix the pillows around me, her hands touching me like little islands of heat.

Lauren's hands continue to explore. Her fingers caress my chest, mapping out the way my ribs twist more to the right than to the left, leaving a sort of dent below the left ribcage. As she scrapes my right nipple, a gasp is pumped out of my chest.

"*Lauren...*" I'm so hard it's literally painful. She *must* be noticing it, even if this part of me is still covered.

Lauren circles the nipple with her finger, flicks the hard nub repeatedly, making me whimper. Then she sits back on her heels, our quick breaths filling the room. "You're perfect," she states, not for the first time.

I don't answer, both because I can't and because I wouldn't know what to say. It's not something I'll ever truly understand, I think.

She leans forward and her thumb strokes over my tight left fist that is pressed to my chest, the motion gentle and definitely loving, until my arm slips away from her, flitting through the air.

I inhale shakily, summoning the remaining control over my muscles that is hiding somewhere. "Kiss me," I whisper. I turn my head slowly, keeping it somewhat still, and Lauren's lips seal with mine. The tip of her tongue worms in between my lips, carefully probing, and licking away at whatever insecurities have been trying to climb out of the pit I shoved them into. Encouraged, I manage to lift my right arm high enough that I can hook my wrist behind her neck and pull her down to me with what little force I manage to apply.

Lauren moans and deepens the kiss, cradling and steadying my head in her hands when it jerks somewhat as her tongue roams along my teeth and tickles the roof of my mouth.

"I'm very glad you came to visit," Lauren whispers close to my face as we part. "I know it wasn't easy for you and I'm so grateful. You're amazing."

My right arm has fallen back on the mattress and is jittering near her thigh. I look away from it and into Lauren's eyes. "I'd do it again," I say slowly, my speech still vastly slurred. "Any time.

As many times as necessary."

And this, by itself, is probably the greatest proof of love I can give her. Because as it turned out, flying to Australia in my condition is the most annoying, painful and exhausting thing you can imagine. I'd rather have lobster for breakfast for the rest of my life than repeat the experience.

Lauren waits until a spasm tipping my head back into the pillow has passed. Her left hand finds mine, slowly threading her fingers with my twisted, trembling ones while her right hand wanders down my chest again, slipping under the blanket. "I wanted this, all of this, since the first moment you came into the hall at the conference. Do you remember?"

I can't talk because her fingertips have stopped at the imaginary line where my shorts would be, so close to my pulsing cock that I don't dare to breathe to avoid unsettling my body and being thrown into another spasm attack. Warm blood pumps through my veins as I blink at Lauren, conveying I remember every bit of our first encounter just as detailed as she does.

"I almost died watching you give the talk and I very nearly did when you answered the questions afterward. Your confidence, your wit, your appearance, everything that is you... geez, it was all so hot to me! I was sure you wouldn't give a damn about me, an inexperienced scientist working at the other end of the world with barely any reputation. I only came forward after almost everyone had already left, because it took all my courage to talk to you, did you know that?"

No, in fact I didn't. It catches me by surprise, because Lauren doesn't seem like a person who has difficulties approaching anyone.

"You were not only damn intelligent. You turned out to be the kindest, funniest man I've ever met. You made me believe in myself again. And gosh, you're the sexiest guy on earth to me. Yes, don't object." She giggles, we've discussed this before, but she catches herself and fixes her gaze back on me. "Well... I just want you to understand that your visit was all I dreamed about for weeks. Next time it will be me flying over to the US, for a much longer time, hopefully." At that, she pulls the rest of the blanket off of me. "And if you make me wait for another second, by the way, I'll literally explode."

I see the familiar twinkle in her eyes, the corners of her mouth twitching in the attempt to hide a smile and I can't help but grin.

This girl...

"Romina won't like it..." I say drily.

Lauren lifts her eyebrows.

"She hates having to clean up after me, she won't tolerate having to clean up when you... you know. Explode."

Lauren's eyes narrow. "Shut up, you're talking too much," she admonishes playfully and laughs when she catches my disbelieving stare at her words. No one ever gets to say I talk too much!

"Touch me."

I know the game by now and when I nod she leads my reluctant right hand to her chest. I gasp slightly when the perfect roundness and softness of one of her breasts is pushed into my palm. After a few seconds I can feel the onset of a spasm and the fear of hurting her by accident is almost too much.

"Lauren..."

My body decides for itself, my fingers twitching and my hand squeezing slightly, and I stare at Lauren in horror as she hisses and closes her eyes.

"Again," she whispers to my surprise.

Exhaling slowly, I concentrate on my right hand and try to repeat the motion, with as much care as if my powerchair was teetering on the edge of a highway and that hand on the joystick the only thing preventing me from running straight into the howling traffic.

"Oh fuck..."

I'm not sure I actually managed any movement, but for Lauren it doesn't seem to matter. I want to tell her that she looks amazing, with the dark brown hair falling into her face and her pink lips slightly open, but all I manage is a weak whisper she can't possibly understand. Lauren, however, smiles as if she knows and closes her eyes, leading my right hand slowly down her front. My knuckles glide over her small belly and between her legs, and Lauren gasps, her hips canting.

"Patrick... holy shit!"

I was wrong in thinking that I'm at best a passive partner during intercourse. The last days have taught me that for Lauren I can be much more than that. I have no idea how I keep my hand in the same position for such a prolonged time, the muscles in my arm straining and quivering, but I must be doing something right because Lauren falls apart within seconds. I dearly hope Romina really went to grab a couple of drinks in the hotel bar because Lauren can be damn loud.

By the time I lose the battle and my arm goes flying we are both panting and flushed. Lauren's hair is flying wild, some strands are matted to her glistening face, and her smile is equal parts coy and dopey. My jaw is locked and the left side of my body is rigid and hurting, but that's nothing against the pain of a rock hard, neglected cock.

Fortunately for me, Lauren finally takes pity. She leans down to me, her scent becoming powerful and intoxicating, her lips trailing against my cheek. "Fuck me," she whispers.

And hell, I can't, not really. But that is a mere technicality the moment Lauren sinks down on me, her face pure wonder and bliss, her beautiful hips entirely making up for the lack of coordinated movement of mine, and when, feverish minutes later, both our breaths stop in the second before reaching the peak, it becomes absolutely insignificant.

As we are lying naked on top of the sheets, drenched in sweat and catching our breaths, Lauren turns her head to look over to me. She stays completely still except for her chest heaving, her eyes resting on me, and I notice that, right now, she's as speechless as I am.

But, luckily, not for very long.

ACKNOWLEDGEMENT

Claiming I published this book on my own would be a blatant lie. Throughout the entire process, from the first draft to the actual publication, so many wonderful, kind and smart people were involved. Thanks in particular to the great Annabelle Costa, for reading the first draft and almost burning her food in the process, for her invaluable professional advice and enthusiasm that propelled this publication forward. A huge thanks to the impossibly talented Rowan who created the steamiest art and cheered for every chapter. I can't thank Lucy May Lennox enough, for her patience and dedication, for the incredible work she put into mending my butchered English, straightening out the kinks and creases in the story, and for giving me the push I urgently needed. Last but not least, I want to thank the paradevo community, in particular Vanessa, Marisa, Sarah and Nessa, who swooped in to help with the arduous work of editing, and everyone who read and commented on my stories, especially those who suggested I publish this one. This book wouldn't exist without you! Thanks for your companionship and continue to be awesome!

Made in the USA
Middletown, DE
13 March 2024

51414541R00099